WITHDRAWN

Dam

Ja

D0356706

BOOK 4

GHOST HUNTRESS
the counseling

MARLEY GIBSON

G RAPHIA

Houghton Mifflin Harcourt
Boston   New York   2010

Copyright © 2010 by Marley Gibson

All rights reserved. Published in the United States by Graphia,
an imprint of Houghton Mifflin Harcourt Publishing Company.

For information about permission to reproduce selections from this book,
write to Permissions, Houghton Mifflin Harcourt Publishing Company,
215 Park Avenue South, New York, New York 10003.

Graphia and the Graphia logo are registered trademarks of
Houghton Mifflin Harcourt Publishing Company.

www.hmhbooks.com

Text set in Bembo.

Library of Congress Cataloging-in-Publication Data

Gibson, Marley.

The counseling / written by Marley Gibson.

p. cm. — (Ghost huntress ; bk. 4)

Summary: On spring break in California, seventeen-year-old psychic Kendall
attends a camp where young people with gifts like hers hone their skills, but she
finds more restless spirits there, as well as the boy from her last vision.

ISBN 978-0-547-39307-0

[1. Psychic ability—Fiction. 2. Ghosts—Fiction. 3. Camps—Fiction. 4.
California—Fiction.] I. Title.

PZ7.G345Cou 2010

[Fic]—dc22

2010009055

Manufactured in the United States of America

DOM 10 9 8 7 6 5 4 3 2 1
4500243137

ACKNOWLEDGMENTS

Thanks so much to Julia Richardson and everyone at Houghton Mifflin Harcourt for continuing to believe in this series. To Deidre Knight, agent extraordinaire, for always taking such good care of me. Thanks to Sean Daily at Hotchkiss and Associates for selling the movie option to Shoulderhill Entertainment.

To Patrick Burns, the absolute love of my life and the inspiration for Patrick Lynn in this book. I hope I did justice to the character. Thank you for rocking my world.

To Wendy Toliver for cheering me on and encouraging me, telling me I can meet my deadline even with Christmas, my birthday, and New Year's smack at the end of it.

To the people who participated in the Darkness Radio Event auction to have characters named for them—Mary McCay and Evan Christian Vanderpoel, or rather their relatives who wanted to see their names in print. Thank you for supporting Erin Gray's Haven House.

To Tiffany Johnson for giving me a copy of her awesome book to use as a reference and guide for my fictional teenagers going through their enlightenment retreat.

To all my fans—especially those in the Philippines, where I'm on the bestseller list—for loving the characters and the story, and for continuing to read. Please keep the e-mails coming.

And to Chris Barton for making my Web presence rock.

Finally, a jumbled thanks to Kathy, Malcolm, Cameron, Errol, and Speedy Wilson; Fran Spencer; Donn Shy; Jen Brown; Melissa Sehgal; Dawn Epright; Arlene Gontz; Susan Cummins; Marlo Scott; Mark and Barbara Nelson; Nina and Jeff Johnson; Andrea Caminiti Norwich; Eric, Jess, and Amy from Sepia Radio; Father Andrew Calder; Evie Haile; John Zaffis; Peggy Armer; Heidi Harman ("You ate it!"); Robbie Thomas; Stacey Jones; Shannon and Jeff Sylvia (and Jacky and Meadow); Rob Hansen; Steve Gonsalves; Jessica Andersen; Charlene Glatkowski; Pam Claughton; Megan Bremer; and, always, Maureen Wood and Ron Kolek.

To the greatest man I've ever known:
he's a husband, father, grandfather, mechanical engineer,
farmer, World War II and Korean War veteran,
comedian, big-time 'Bama football fan (Roll Tide!),
and the best daddy a girl could ever ask for—
Joseph Eve "Joe" Harbuck Jr.

At any given moment life is completely senseless. But viewed over a period, it seems to reveal itself as an organism existing in time, having a purpose, tending in a certain direction.

—Aldous Huxley

Chapter One

THERE'S A SAYING IN THE SOUTH that if you go to heaven or hell, you have to go through the freakin' Atlanta airport first.

For me, though, blowing off the dust of my new hometown of Radisson, Georgia, the Hartsfield-Jackson Atlanta International Airport is the gateway to new possibilities. I'm setting off on my spring break adventure. Besides, with all that's happened to me recently—going through my psychic awakening; having a near-death experience; losing my boyfriend, Jason, and one of my best friends, Taylor, to the wilds of Alaska; and now these recurring dreams of a mystery guy I call Hershey Eyes—dude, I need a Total Life Break.

"You don't have a Diet Coke stashed in your backpack, do you, Kendall? You know they'll just take it from you," my mom says as we stand outside the nylon-strap spaghetti maze that is TSA airport security.

I pull the half-finished twenty-ouncer from my purse and hand it over to my mother. Well, not my *real* mother, as I just recently found out. Sarah and David Moorehead are my adoptive parents; my birth mother, Emily, my former spirit guide, died minutes after I was born, seventeen years ago. I haven't had time to find out more info on her, but I will eventually.

Dad rubs the back of my neck as I cram my trial-size bottle of hairspray, mini toothpaste, Carmex, and hand sanitizer into the airport-approved plastic Ziploc bag. "We're going to miss you, kiddo," he says affectionately.

"I'll miss you guys too."

Mom sniffs the tears that are gathering. "I don't know what to do for a week with both of my girls gone." My little sister, Kaitlin, is in Florida for soccer camp, so the Moorehead nest will be empty for seven days.

"Please don't forget to feed the cats," I say. "Natalie won't eat the dry food, and Eleanor won't eat the wet food. Buckley will eat all of it, so make sure everyone gets some. And water. They need a lot of water so they won't get little kitty urinary tract infections."

My mom the nurse clicks her tongue. "I'm perfectly capable of caring for your cats. You focus on you, dear."

I chuckle in spite of myself. Of course she knows what to do. "Check in on Loreen too, would you? Just to make sure she's okay."

Now it's Mom's turn to laugh. "Honey, Loreen is in good hands with Father Massimo. Those two are inseparable." I have to admit, I saw *that* one coming. My Episcopal priest and my psychic mentor. They make quite an . . . eclectic pair.

"If anyone deserves a nice getaway, it's you, Kendall," Dad adds with a tug on my long hair.

"Tru' dat, Dad."

Seeing as how my last ghost-hunting effort ended up with me in a hospital bed minus a spleen and plus a reinflated lung and a blood transfusion from my best friend, I definitely need a break, spring or otherwise. Okay, so I got the bitter spirit at the mayor's mansion to finally pass into the light and everything was all right in the end, but g'friend here needs a breather from both Radisson and investigating entities in people's homes. This whole psychic awakening has finally discombobulated me with a visit to "heaven" and a chat with my dead grandma. I don't know which way to turn anymore. I don't know if what I'm seeing, feeling, hearing, or experiencing is from me or from someone else. I have to get control. So here I am at the airport: laptop, books, BlackBerry, and Sonoma the bear in my backpack, one extremely large rolly bag checked in, ready to board a Delta flight to Fresno, California, for ... *whatever* ... awaits me there.

"Yo, K, fancy meeting you here!" someone calls out to me.

The gangly, tall black-haired girl with the familiar smiling face bounds up to me, a humongoid tote bag hitched over her left shoulder.

"Nichols! I thought you were going ahead to Tybee Island without me," I say to my best friend and fellow ghost huntress, Celia. No, she's more than that. We're blood sisters, now that her life-saving transfusion is flowing through my veins.

"Change of plans," Celia tells me. "Dad got a call this morning asking him to keynote at this retailers' convention, so I decided to blow off Tybee and tag along with the parentals."

Ah, the founder of Mega-Mart—that's a real no-brainer.

"Didn't you get my text?" she asks. "I figured I'd run into you here."

I glance at my BlackBerry. "Nope. *Nada.*" Hmm . . . nothing from Celia. Nothing from anyone, for that matter, although I'm trying not to dwell on the loss of Jason Tillson in my life.

"Well, get this," Celia says, lifting her eyes to mine. "I thought I'd take advantage of the locale of Daddyo's conference to do some more research. I'm going to plop my paranormal-investigator self into the Windy City and continue trying to find out just who Emily Jane Faulkner was, other than your birth mother."

I swallow hard. "You're going to Chicago?" My Chicago? Man, I wish I could refresh myself at the altar of the Mag Mile, go to Navy Pier, get an authentic red-hot, and take a walk along Lake Michigan. With all the things that have happened since my psychic awakening, there's a part of me that longs for the simpler days of when I lived on the Gold Coast. When I didn't see and hear spirits. When I wasn't physically harmed by them. And when my heart wasn't broken by a guy with gorgeous blue eyes. I shake loose from feeling sorry for myself and force a smile. "Where are you staying?"

Celia shrugs and says, "The Fairmont."

I quirk a smirk at her. "Welllll . . . excuse me," I say with a laugh.

She smiles. "That's how we Nicholses roll."

Dad puts his hand on my shoulder and tells Celia, "You must have dinner at the Chop House. Best steaks in town."

"Cool. I'll remember that, Mr. David."

Celia's mother appears behind Celia and turns a smile on me. "Where is it you're going again, dear?"

A deep sigh escapes from me. It's not like I don't want to go on this trip. It's just more of the fear of the unknown and unexpected. You'd think a psychic could see more clearly into her own future, but that's not the case with me. I'm much more in tune with other people's lives. I get snippets and clues of things in my dreams—like meeting Jason and even being pushed down the staircase by the mayor's ghost—but I never know what's a premonition and what's just a brain dump or an overactive imagination.

I adjust my bag on my shoulder and shift my weight between feet. "Mom registered me for this exclusive-like Enlightened Youth Retreat in Oakbriar, California, that's hosted by that guy Oliver Bates, from TV."

Celia's eyes pop wide. *"Ethereal Evidence,"* she interjects, nearly breathless. "You know the show, Mom. I've got every episode on my DVR."

Mrs. Nichols waves her hand. "Oh, now, Celia. I can't keep up with all the TV programs you kids watch."

Celia rolls her eyes at her mother and then turns to me. "I told you, the guy is amazing. He nails everything on that show. Nothing gets past him. You're gonna have an awesome time!"

I haven't watched nearly as many paranormal shows as

Celia—who can keep up with all of them—so I just lift my brows at her in recognition. "Yeah, that's what the brochure says."

"So what do you know about the week's agenda?" she presses. "Are you sleeping in tents and toasting marshmallows while singing 'Kumbaya'?"

I stick my tongue out at her for her cheekiness. "No, I told you, it's for kids like me with 'special abilities.' It looks a little chichi from the brochure, so I'll just have to wait and see." Everything's happened so quickly that I haven't really had a chance to tell her more than the basics. We've barely had time to accept that Jason and Taylor Tillson have moved off to Alaska, and our sun-and-sand time in Tybee together had to be canceled. "Dr. Kindberg, the shrink I saw in Atlanta, pulled some strings and got me into this latest session just under the wire."

Celia winks. "Gotta love those strings."

"I suppose so," I say with a snicker. "Looks like we'll have all sorts of sessions with counselors to discuss our abilities and hone them. Mostly, it'll be good to meet other people who are . . . like me." What exactly would that be? Psychic? Adopted? Confused? All of the above?

"Well, you totally have to get me Oliver Bates's autograph," Celia says. "Oh, and tell him I love his show and I'm his biggest fan!"

Mr. Nichols arrives and interrupts us. "We need to get through security if we're going to make our flight, Celia."

"Sure thing, Dad."

"Me too," I say.

Celia and her parents move toward the security line after saying goodbye to my folks. I wait a moment, standing stock-still as my heart beats a hundred times a minute. This is a big step for me. I'm seventeen and flying by myself for the first time—I hope the airline doesn't, like, have an escort for me, a Delta coloring book, and wings for me to wear. If I can deal with seeing, hearing, and speaking to spirits, I think I can handle a six-hour flight west on my own without incident. Thing is, all I've known for these past seventeen years has been turned topsy-turvy and I feel like I'm at a point of starting over and really finding myself.

Mom must sense this, even though she's not psychic like I am. She pulls me to her chest and squeezes me tightly. I wrap my arms around her waist and close my eyes. She may not have physically given birth to me, but she has raised me and she *is* my mother. She *chose* me. That has to mean something. "I love you, Kendall. I hope this trip helps you, sweetie."

I cling to her safety and warmth as I gather my strength. "Thanks, Mom. Me too."

Dad nudges us apart and places a peck on my forehead. "Call us when you touch down in Fresno, kiddo."

"Will do, Dad. Love ya; mean it!"

I blow kisses and hustle forward to join Celia and her parents going through security. Remarkably, the line moves quickly and I pass the ultraviolet flashlight test over my driver's license done by the guy in the royal blue shirt. I strip off my belt and my footwear at the TSA checkpoint (ewww—how many viruses and fungi live in that allegedly disposable antimicrobial carpet that doesn't appear to have been disposed of since 9/11?) and place my laptop in a separate bin. Celia does the same and then calls over her shoulder to me.

"You have to text and e-mail and call and keep me posted on your retreat."

"Oh, you know I will," I say, rezipping my backpack so Sonoma the bear doesn't fall out going across the belt and through the scanner. "And you have to keep me posted on what's going on in Chicago."

Celia's dark eyes grow serious. "I'm going to find out all I can about Emily, K. I promise. My cousin Paul is still working on leads from the Wisconsin plate you had in your vision."

"Thanks, Cel." I swallow the sudden emotional lump in my throat as I think of my real mother, who died so young on a cold, rainy December night in Chicago. "I appreciate your diligence."

"You'd do the same for me if I were in your shoes," she says. Then she looks down at our feet. "Well . . . your bare feet."

We laugh together and it feels really good. I'm blessed to have a neighbor and friend like Celia Nichols, a girl who welcomed me to Radisson with open arms and accepts me for who I've become. What that is, I'm still trying to find out. This retreat *has* to help.

"You're the best, Cel."

She nods. "Yep. I am."

We reassemble ourselves after our bags clear the belts and head down the escalator to the tram that will take us to our respective terminals. When we near Concourse B, I announce, "This is me."

Celia loops her long arm over my shoulder and squeezes. "You go get enlightened, Kendall, and I'll find out what I can about your family and piece together who the players are: John Thomas and Anna Wynn Faulkner, and whoever this Andy Caminiti was . . . or is."

My chest aches at the names of my possible grandparents, who I saw in a vision, along with the Wisconsin license plate of Emily's destroyed car. And who is Andy Caminiti? The name I got in a vision. Did he die in the car crash with Emily? Is he alive? Is he my father? Does he know my father? Does he know *anything*?

I sigh. So many questions. So few answers. But at least Celia's trying for me.

The tram stops and the electronic voice announces my terminal. With a final grip of hands, Celia and I separate, and I step off. The doors close between us and she waves at me, then continues on her way.

I follow the stream of passengers up the slow-moving escalator, all of them going to different destinations for various reasons. My psychic senses suddenly click in with awareness of the people around me. A near buzz of information encircles my head. The woman in red in front of me is going to a Mary Kay conference in Buffalo. The fat businessman in the custom-made suit is flying to see his mistress at the airport Holiday Inn in Louisville—classssssssssy; not, especially since I know he's got a wife and three daughters at home. The older couple behind me is going to the funeral of a friend in Dallas who died after a failed triple bypass. So much sadness, remorse, guilt, and anxiety. Emotions fly around, as thick in here as the airplanes are outside.

And then there's me. The psychic girl who's gained and lost so much and needs direction in her life. The one who is off to California where she hopes to find . . . meaning for her psychic abilities and how she can move forward from a freaky near-death experience.

Okay . . . so it's not a funeral or an affair, but it's emotional enough for me.

I take a deep breath as I step off the escalator and turn right in search of my gate and the plane that will wing me to the Left Coast in search of answers. I need to tamp down the angst and be open-minded about what lies ahead for me. Particularly, about meeting other people who are like me. *Kids* who are like me. And experienced adults who want to help, teach, and counsel. Enlightened guides who want to lead me in the direction I'm meant to go in. Whatever that is.

In six hours, when flight number 1518 touches down, I'll find out.

CHAPTER TWO

FOLLOWING THE REQUISITE SAFETY REVIEW, the takeoff, a can of Mr. and Mrs. T's bloody mary mix (sans alcohol, thankyou-verymuch), and some mini pretzels, I adjust in seat 11A and try to center my thoughts, to focus on my breathing and not . . . dwell on anything. Fortunately, seats 11B and 11C are empty, so once I make a quick run to the potty chamber—after the captain extinguishes the seat-belt sign—I'm going to stretch out and zzz my way into Cali.

When I get back from the bathroom, though, a man who wasn't there before is sitting in the aisle seat of my row. Maybe he moved after takeoff for more legroom or what have you.

"Sorry, sir, may I get back in?"

He doesn't look at me, just stares ahead blankly. He's dressed in nicely pressed khakis and a blue and white thin-striped button-down, like he's going to a trade show or it's business-casual Friday for him. Where was he sitting before? I wonder.

The flight attendant stops in front of me. "You may want to take your seat. The captain says we're going to have some choppy air up ahead."

"Sure thing," I say, not wanting to go against her authority. "Just waiting for him to let me pass into the row."

The woman looks at the adjoining seats and then back at me. "You're waiting for who?"

I glance at him.

I glance at her.

It all clicks.

My ears ring and my heart rate picks up. *Not so soon* . . .

My psychic headache begins to tick away at my right temple and I realize that the dressed-for-work man in 11C is . . . not a ticketed passenger. At least, not on this flight.

He's a ghost.

With that, the man twists his head up and winks at me.

Sigh. *Here I go again* . . .

I shake my head at the flight attendant. "Sorry, I'll take my seat."

She smiles warmly, but I can read her thoughts, and she thinks I'm a silly teenager. I wish it were merely that. Right now, there's a spirit who's in need of my attention whether I want to give it to him or not. These damn ghosts will follow me anywhere, won't they?

Taking a bold step, I walk straight through the man in 11C like he's a wispy cloud and sit down. "Hey," I say softly without peeking over at him.

"This flight is taking forever," he says to me. "Do you know what time we're going to land?"

"Where are you going?" I ask.

He glances at his watch. "I've got to get to the West Coast office. A new server's going in and they're expecting me."

I breathe in, picking up his energies, which are crackling around me like fireflies on a July night. Information is tossed at me like beanbags, and I mentally try to catch all I can and sort it out as the headache pings away above my right eye. This guy works in tech support for a company with bicoastal offices. He's from . . . Lawrenceville, Georgia. Other images flash before me. "Is your name . . . Richard?" I ask, because I see the image of President Nixon in my head for some reason. Don't ask me to explain how my psychic images work. They just do.

"Richard Newman. I go by Richie," the man says.

"Kendall," I say in a whisper even though we could carry on this conversation without words. "Nice to meet you." When he extends his hand, I politely lift mine, although there's no physical contact between us. I watch as his fingers blend into mine, disappearing into my skin with his attempt to grip and shake. This doesn't seem to faze him.

"Do you know what happened to you?" I press.

"What do you mean?"

I scrunch up my face. "Like, why you're here?"

He stares at me blankly, unknowingly. Possibly perplexed.

His dark hair is short and spiked and his face shows his confusion over the situation. "I left early for the airport and caught my flight to Oakland. I don't understand why we're not there yet. The captain hasn't said anything about a delay and I can't get any of the flight attendants to answer my call button. I'm going to get my ass chewed if I don't get to the office."

Poor guy doesn't even know he's passed.

Concentrating on the spirit next to me, I continue to breathe in deeply and open myself up to the energies all around. I reach my hand over to where he's sitting and I fan my fingers about to connect with him the best I can. Now, without speaking, our minds bond and he shows me his last day.

Richie took MARTA from his house in Lawrenceville to the Atlanta airport a week ago and hopped this exact plane to take him to Oakland, California. Following drink service and a perusal of a story about the High-Stickin' Chickens' (my name for the Atlanta Thrashers hockey team) victory over my Chicago Blackhawks (damnit!), Richie got up to go to the restroom and suddenly felt an intense pain. I feel it now myself, searing across my middle.

"Your stomach hurt, didn't it?"

"Yeah, how did you know?" he asks with surprise in his eyes.

"I just do. It's sort of . . . my thing."

"It was an awful cramp," he says. "I'm fine now, but it hurt like hell for a while. I thought it was just my thirty-five-year-old body reacting to the weekend's softball game. Man, we got our asses kicked."

I laugh softly. "What happened in the game?"

Richie shares the memory with me. "I was on first and Arredondo was at bat. Hit the hell out of it to clean the bases. I rounded third and felt the ball coming back in, so I kicked in the afterburners and slid. Got a raspberry on my thigh to end all bruises. And I remember feeling like I tore a muscle in my stomach or something. Dude tagged me out, so I was more pissed off about that."

I inhale deeply and stretch my hands out again, trying to connect with this spirit as much as I can. In my mind's eye, I see nothing but blood. Seeping. Slowly. Internal damage unknown to the man himself. Slumping in my seat, I ponder how to approach this, especially since he doesn't realize he's passed.

But Richie turns to me. "It was more, though, wasn't it?"

I smile feebly at him, but it becomes a frown because I can see ever so clearly what happened. This is what being a psychic/empath is all about. I want to cry at being the one who has to tell this guy that he's, like, dead. All part of the burden of my so-called gift.

"Richie," I say out loud. "I have something to tell you." Then I reach my hand across the empty seat between us, as if that's going to add any comfort. "You tore your abdominal muscle and it went unattended. You were slowly bleeding to death and didn't even know it until you collapsed. Right here on this very plane. Another passenger knew CPR and tried to revive you as the pilot made an emergency landing in Dallas."

I watch a crawling acceptance come across Richie's tan face. "Man, that sucks."

"Yeah, it does."

Richie stares ahead at the seat in front of him, his jaw slack in disbelief. It's best that I leave him alone until he wants to talk further. He needs time for this to soak in. About fifteen minutes later for me—perhaps a lifetime or a nanosecond for him—Richie turns. "I can't be dead," he says. "I just got paid. I've got a mortgage, and I'm getting married in a few months."

He puts his head in his hands and runs his fingers through his short-cropped hair. A young woman with a bright smile comes into my vision. Her high ponytail swings left and right as she laughs at something Richie said to her. Her name is Lindsey. The sparkle on her left hand tells me that she's the one he intended to marry. Tears well up behind my eyes as I think of his fiancée moving on without him. Now I need to help him move on.

Sitting back, he lets out a frustrated sigh. "I remember now. All of it. I knew I was dying. I didn't make it to the hospital, did I?"

I bite down on my bottom lip and try to tune in to the residual energy left here on this aircraft. "I believe the man who helped you revived you enough to get you off the plane and to the hospital. But you never woke up there."

"Damn. That totally sucks."

Acceptance seems to wash over him like a gentle breeze.

"You know you can't, like, stay on this plane forever, right?"

Richie slowly nods his head and then sits up.

"Have you seen the light, Richie?"

He nods again. "It's been around for a while. I just didn't know what it was."

"Do you see it now? Where is it?"

Richie points forward. "Up there. How do I, umm, you know, go to it?"

"You just do," I tell him. "Focus on it and let it absorb you."

"Just like that?"

I smile weakly. "Just like that."

"What about my girl?" he asks. "She has to know how much I loved her. How much I wanted to spend the rest of my life with her. Have babies. Get a dog and a cat. All the stuff you're supposed to do. I've also got her wedding gift stashed in the attic of the house. It's a black pearl necklace I got off eBay from the family of a World War Two veteran who picked it up in Japan in the 1940s. Lindsey loves pearls, and these are the most gorgeous ones ever."

My heart almost stops for a moment over the love I sense from Richie for his fiancée. "Wow. That's an amazing gift that doesn't need to be lost." I gulp the emotional knob in my throat. I don't want to ask this question, but it's what I have to do. What I've done so many times. "Is there anything I can do?"

He looks around and lets out a long sigh. "Can you tell her about the necklace?"

"I-I-I guess I can." What? Walk up to her house, knock on the door, and relate this tête-à-tête to her?

"Yeah, exactly," he says with a smile, obviously hearing my thoughts. "And tell her something else for me, would you?"

Reluctantly, I nab my small notebook from my purse and make a few notes of what Richie wants me to tell Lindsey. I write down her address in Lawrenceville and her work information and all of the love-inspired things Richie tells me. He stops talking and relays the special message of ultimate love for his fiancée. Hot tears jet from my eyes as my heart throbs for Richie and Lindsey's loss. I write down his exact words, wondering how in the world I can convey them to the grieving woman with the same emotional impact as Richie.

"You'll make sure you get all of this to her?" he implores.

"I will," I say out loud, not knowing how or when I'll make it to her house or if this poor mourning woman will slam the door in my face and tell me to get lost. I wipe the tears from my eyes, hoping my makeup isn't streaked and running down my cheeks. "I'll do my best."

He winks at me again. "You're a good kid, Kendall. Don't forget that."

Richie stands, walks down the aisle of the plane, and . . . disappears. I gasp at what I witness. It never fails to stir my emotions when a ghost moves into the light and becomes a free spirit. Three more salty tears escape my eyes and I push them aside into my hair. I also let a sigh of relief leave my lungs in a pent-up breath. Worry coats me in an unfashionable garb. If only all of the spirits I connect with could be as amenable and affable as Richie. But there are bad elements out there. Entities that are bitter and hateful . . . and hurtful. Those are the ones I can't deal with anymore. How can I know, though, going into it? I hope Oliver Bates and his counselors have an answer for me on how to live my life moving forward. Being psychic is the hand of cards I've been dealt and I have to deal with it. Bad card pun aside.

I let out another long sigh and then I feel a set of eyes on me. The older man across the aisle is glaring at me like I'm a complete idiot. His harsh, overgrown brows are knitted together and he presses his lips into a grimace.

"Young lady, is there something wrong with you?" he asks, obviously referring to my convo with no one that he could see.

"Mister," I say with my mouth hitched to the side, "you have *no* idea."

When my plane touches down in Fresno, I have my emotions in check. At least for the moment. The two-hour crash nap—shouldn't really say *crash* when I'm on an airplane—did me a world of good. I stretch my limbs, rub my eyes, and sit up straight as I wait to deplane. California. West Coast. A different environment. My spring break has officially begun; here I go. The attention now is on this retreat and rediscovering who Kendall Moorehead is and who she needs to be.

Ack . . . why am I referring to myself in the third person?

Following a quick potty stop and a call home to let them know I landed safely, I dash through the terminal to baggage claim to get my gray Kenneth Cole bag off the belt. As the conglomeration of suitcases passes by, I take a quick glance through the itinerary I printed from my confirmation e-mail for the retreat. According to the info, a sedan will be picking me up outside of baggage claim and driving me to the Rose Briar Inn. It sounds so lovely and peaceful.

With an adroit heft of my exactly-fifty-pound bag, I pull the handle, drag the rolly beast behind me, and search for the exit for ground transportation. I wonder if the sedan driver will be holding a sign that reads KENDALL MOOREHEAD. How cool would *that* be? Like I'm some sort of celebrity showing up for a reality show or—

Oooph!

What the . . . ?

I nearly bust my ass in the middle of the airport but catch myself on my hands before I hit the ground. Phew! I look under me and see that I've fallen over a guitar case that's been left in the walkway. What kind of idiot leaves a guitar out where people can trip over it? The black case is covered in stickers from several cities that the owner must have traveled to, as well as indications of his or her taste in music. I see decals for the Beatles, Rolling Stones, the Doors, Jimmy Buffett, Hall and Oates, Bon Jovi, and Nine Inch Nails. Man, this person is old school when it comes to music.

"Watch where you're going, okay?"

My head snaps up and I snarl, "I wouldn't have to watch where I'm going if you hadn't left your guitar in the middle of the freakin' floor!"

The guy just sits there. A knit cap is over his hair and head-phones encircle his neck. His eyes are covered by dark sun-glasses and I can't make out any touch of emotion on his face. I get up and my mental fingers stretch to connect with what-ever this guy's glitch is, but he's completely unreadable to me. It's like my radar is blocked.

He shifts his long, baggy-jeaned legs and puts his head-phones back in place, mumbling something under his breath.

"Ex*cuse* me?"

"I said, the guitar is personally autographed and a collector's item."

Hands on hips, I cop a 'tude back at him. "Then take better care of it." *Jackass.* With that, I turn and walk off.

The sound of the case shuffling against the floor touches my ears, but I also hear him say "Nice language" in a snarky tone. "You kiss your mother with that mouth?" he calls.

OMG! He totally heard that? I said it in my head! How did he catch it? Yikes! I put the pedal to the metal and power out of the baggage area, away from him and my wicked embarrass-ment. Making one last turn, I see him delve into a *Popular Mechanics* magazine as if I were never there.

There's something familiar about him ... only ... not. Must be my psychic energies suffering from jet lag.

I burst into the bright California sunshine and search for the sedan or a sign with my name on it. Thank God I'll never have to run into Mr. Attitude *ever* again.

CHAPTER THREE

A TALL ITALIAN-LOOKING MAN in a finely tailored suit stands outside of a shiny black limo holding a sign that reads MOORE-HEAD.

"Is this seriously for me?" I squeak out. I've never ridden in a limo in my life!

"You are Miss Moorehead?"

Trying to make light of it all, I say, "The one and only."

He drops the sign to the hood of the car and swiftly moves to take my suitcase from me. I let him tug it out of my hand; my Spidey senses tell me he's not some vagrant posing in a designer suit just to steal my week's worth of clothing and vitamins.

"Welcome to California. I am Sergio and I am here to drive you to the Rose Briar Inn." He grabs the handle of the limo's rear door, opens it, and waves his hand as if to present the limo to me. I poke my head inside and then slip into the seat.

Whoa. Someone pinch me 'cause I think I'm dreaming.

From the looks of this luxury whip, Oliver Bates knows how to pamper his guests, that's for sure. This retreat must have set Mom and Dad back a pretty penny, with amenities like this.

Sergio closes the door behind me and I hear him stashing my bag in the trunk. I let out a long whistle as I take in my surroundings. Not exactly Mom's twelve-year-old Volvo. The leather interior smells earthy and expensive. I squiggle my butt around to get comfortable and relax into the cushion. A plush red carpet spreads out under my feet. To the left, the bench seat curves around, enough room to hold at least ten people. On the right is a wet bar and a small television. A silver bucket of ice holds designer-label bottles of water; a crystal glass is poised on each side. Next to that is a ginormous basket with apples, grapes, oranges, and granola bars of all flavors.

Sergio rolls down the dividing window between the two of us and flashes a perfectly capped white grin at me. "Are you ready to go now, Miss Moorehead?"

"Umm, sure."

Are you kidding me? I get this limo all to myself? Celia's never going to believe this. I snap a few pics with my cell phone camera just to prove it to her later.

Before I know it, we're maneuvering out of the airport and buzzing up Route 41. Traffic is remarkably light—considering all the horror stories you hear about California highways—so I stretch my legs out and take in the scenery of Fresno that's flying by outside the tinted windows.

The TV blinks awake and I see Oliver Bates from *Ethereal Evidence* smiling at me. "Welcome to the Enlightened Youth Retreat," he says. "I'm Oliver Bates, your host for the next week. I'm a psychic/medium/sensitive and I'm here to teach you all I know about your higher self and being in touch with the earth elements and the powers you can harness from the metaphysical realm." He continues on to discuss the itinerary for the week ahead, but I sort of tune out as I stare at the screen. Oliver has sunglasses perched on dark brown hair, and his nearly black eyes shine. His hand reaches up to twist his jet-black mustache, much like he does on TV when he's getting the psychic messages from beyond that help him assist police with cold-case homicides and finding missing persons. I can't believe I'm actually going to meet him. I've never met anyone *famous* before. Unless you count the time that I saw Michael Jordan going into the Chicago Tribune Tower on Michigan Avenue when I was eight years old.

As Oliver continues his welcoming video, I reach over and pour myself a sparkly-dancing glass of San Pellegrino and take a long, enjoyable sip as we speed toward my destination.

Now I'm not so jealous of Celia in Chicago at the Fairmont.

"We're here, Miss Moorehead."

Sergio's accent breaks into the haze of my sleepiness. I sit up in time to hear the tires of the limo crunching over the gravelly driveway of the Rose Briar Inn. I pull my hands through my hair and then rub the back of my index finger under my eyes to wipe away the sleep. Man, winging it to the Wrong Coast totally kicked my rear heinie. I hope I didn't drool or snore or anything like that.

I gather my purse and backpack, and when Sergio opens the door, I scoot out into the ultra-bright California sunshine. He has my suitcase and leads me up the stone pathway to the enormous covered veranda of the manor house. He puts down my bag and leaves. In my peripherals, I see a tabby cat scurry into the bushes, followed by a calico one. I climb the three rock stairs up to the porch and stand next to where Sergio has left my bag.

Yip! Yip! Yip!

Down by my feet is a yappy orange and white dog. His pink tongue lolls to the side as he looks up at me with his remarkably large eyes.

"Hey, boy!" I say, squatting down to his level. His bushy tail waves back and forth like nobody's business and he twists and turns in excitement. I reach for his collar and read *Speedy*. "Well, hey there, Speedy. Aren't you precious?"

A lick of my hand confirms that he knows he is indeed special.

"Awww . . . doosk at the pwecious baby. What kind of doggy are you, Sir Speedy?"

"He's a papillon," I hear from above. A woman in her forties wipes her hands on the front of her flowery apron and approaches me with her hand stretched out. "He's my attack dog. He harasses you with licks and puppy kisses. Isn't that right?"

Yip! Yip!

I stand up from my puppy petting and stretch out my hand

to the woman in front of me. "I'm Kendall Moorehead. Here for the retreat. Is this where I check in?" I ask politely.

"Of course it is, hon. That's what I'm here for." Her blue eyes sparkle and I sense nothing but warmth and friendliness from her. "I'm Chris La'Coston. Manager, night clerk, housekeeper, chef, you name it." She pats her short golden hair in pride and motions for me to tag along inside with her.

I grab my suitcase and follow Mrs. La'Coston into the foyer of the massive building and take in my surroundings. I see through a doorway into a large sitting room filled with antique Victorian furniture; there are plump, cushiony couches in an adjoining living room. A roaring fire is going in the fireplace in the sitting room, yet the room isn't unbearably hot. This is *not* your typical bed-and-breakfast. It's like a bed-and-breakfast on steroids. Along the back wall of the sitting room are massive windows and french doors leading out to a balcony. Through the sparkly windows, I can see down to a conglomeration of small cabins, all built into the mountain, and a yard that overlooks the foothills of the Sierra Nevadas. It's times like this that I wish I were a writer and could pen an amazing tome dedicated to the nature and beauty surrounding me. Sadly, all I can say is this place is frickin' awesome.

"Now, which one are you again?" Mrs. La'Coston asks.

"I'm Kendall Moorehead," I repeat.

A phone rings in the distance. "Well, welcome to Rose Briar, Kendall. Let me just grab that call and I'll get you to your room. Glenn's out helping some of the others get settled."

Without having to be told, I know that Glenn is her husband and he helps her run the inn.

I nod and turn my gaze toward the rising green mountains that literally glisten in the sunlight. Either that or Chris La'Coston has some secret cleaning formula that makes the windows crystal clear. Everything is spotless here and the air is so fresh and clean, I get the feeling it must be what rain tastes like.

"Score!" I hear someone shout and I follow the sound through the french doors and out onto the back deck. An expansive green umbrella shades a glass-topped table with black tiles spread all over it. A young boy sits in one of the wide wicker chairs entertaining himself with a set of dominoes.

I drop my purse and backpack onto the settee outside the door and quietly watch him as he works. The tiles all face down and are scattered about like they don't care. The boy's hand hovers over them as he concentrates with his eyes closed, softly muttering numbers.

"Two sixes," he says softly. Then he flips over the tile and, sure enough, he nailed it!

"Way to go!" I say, unable to hold in my cheering.

He jumps slightly when he hears me. When he spins around, I see he can't be more than thirteen, if that. "Oh, didn't know you were there."

"Sorry," I say. "Didn't mean to freak you out."

His eyes shift to the dominoes and then back to me. "I'm sorta jittery these days."

"I know how that is," I say with a sigh. I'm not going to be the only freak ... errr ... gifted one here this week. "Hey, I'm Kendall."

Sitting tall, the boy says, "Evan Christian Vanderpoel, from Long Beach, California."

That's an awfully big-sounding name for such a little guy, but I don't dare say that out loud. When he frowns at me a bit, I sense he must have read my thoughts. Ah, well ... gotta watch that this week.

"Wanna sit?" he asks.

I pull out the chair next to him and plop down.

Chris La'Coston joins us, announcing her presence with a long sigh. "There now, where were we? Oh, right. We need to get you kids your rooms. One sec!" She rotates on a heel and disappears again.

"I can't imagine running this entire place," I note.

"Me either, but then I never woulda imagined myself at a place like this at all," he says.

I swallow hard. "How long since ... your awakening?"

He shrugs like it's no big deal. "I guess I sorta always knew stuff I shouldn't. It helps me with my schoolwork and tests, but it freaks my mom out. She thinks I've got ADHD or something like that 'cause my mind's all over the place. It's hard to concentrate on any one thing. I've got a bunch of pills the doctor gave me."

I sigh along with him. "My mom didn't take my awakening

very well at first, either. I had to do the whole visiting-of-the-shrink thing, complete with blood tests and brain scans. Fortunately, I've avoided medication so far."

He crooks a smile my way. "So have I. I fake taking my pills. Flush a lot of them."

"You go, Evan Christian!"

Speedy joins us on the veranda, waving his fluffy white tail like a flag of surrender. He barks and growls and starts nipping at my new friend's feet. I can see that Evan Christian is a bit uncomfortable with the high-spirited dog, so I invite Speedy to hop up onto my lap. He does willingly, rubbing his bottom against me and flipping over for a tummy rub. I oblige, watching his back left paw shake in delight.

Chris returns with a set of old-fashioned skeleton keys hanging off a long golden cord. "Now, Speedy, don't you bother these teenagers."

"It's no problem," I say, continuing to rub. Speedy flips back over and growls at the mistress of the manor.

She claps her hands at him and says, "Don't you go getting hinky on me, Speedy."

Speedy hops out of my lap and with a derisive grunt trots off to who knows where.

"Come on along," Chris says, waving keys in the air. We follow around the west side of the large inn to a set of cabins lined up. She unlocks the french door and swings it inside. "This here's your room, Evan Christian."

I wait patiently on the path while she flips on lights and escorts him in. There are roses of various colors crawling up a large trellis on the side of the building. Pinks and yellows mix cheerfully with reds and whites. Prickly briars dance around the lovely flowers, a warning not to pick the blooms but just enjoy their beauty and splendor. I breathe in deeply, appreciating the back-to-nature feel of the inn, the majestic mountains providing a scenic backdrop. Oliver Bates couldn't have picked a more magical place to hold his retreat and I'm totally grateful that Mom and Dad sent me here to regroup.

"Okay, now, Kendall. Let's get you settled, sweetheart," Chris says with a wide smile.

We traverse the stone path around to the right, past fenced-in porches and more curtained french doors. The dazzling California sun cuts a guiding light across the ground, leading to cabin 14, where I know Chris will be putting me.

Sure enough, at the door with the glistening gold *14*, Chris La'Coston takes the skeleton key and slips it into the lock with a knowing click.

"All you girls will be staying here on the east side," she tells me.

I gasp when I see into the room. Deep mauves and creams accent the lacy décor of the suite. Two double beds sit to the left of the front door, adorned with hand-sewn quilts and mounds of fluffy pillows. To the right, three steps up, is a small kitchenette. An antique rocking chair sits in the corner next to a wooden coat rack and a chest of drawers. My eyes grow wide when I look to the bathroom area to see not only the essentials of modern facilities, but also a curtained Jacuzzi tub.

"Wow," I manage to get out. "This place is amazing. And my own whirlpool?"

Chris smiles. "Oliver likes for his guests to feel at home."

I don't exactly have my own hot tub at home, but what Oliver Bates doesn't know won't hurt him.

"You get settled in and rest up. I'm sure the time change is affecting you some. When everyone gets here, we'll have a nice cookout so you can all get acquainted," Chris says.

When the door closes behind her, I spin around and around in the room and then flop backwards on the closest bed. I sink into the downy softness and it's like being on a cloud, wrapped in angel's wings. Could this mattress be *any* more comfortable? Can I take it home with me at the end of the week?

"Ahhhhhh," I say to no one and snuggle in, thinking a little more Nappy McNapperton might not be a bad idea after all, to get used to the Pacific time zone.

However, someone doesn't want me to slip into la-la land yet.

Can you help me? whispers out to me.

No. I don't want to hear any more voices today. The guy on the plane totally exhausted me.

Help me . . .

The weight of anxiety presses against my chest and it's difficult to breathe. I squeeze my eyes shut tight, hoping to block out whatever—or whoever—is speaking to me.

Please help me . . .

Nope. Not gonna answer. If I pay it no mind, maybe it'll go away.

My ears begin to ring like church bells on a Sunday morning. I do my best to tamp down not only the familiar headache that comes with my psychic visions but the anxiousness churning through my veins. Is this a good spirit or a bad spirit? Does it want to hurt me? Is it begging for help only so it can lure me in and try to harm me?

I start to pick up the place-memory essence of entities that have been here in the past. Are these spirits of the living or the deceased? I have no way to discern that at the moment, nor do I want to.

Grabbing my MP3 player, I loop my headphones on, crank up a Beyoncé remix, and turn the volume to maximum. I press into the mattress, and with an extra tightening of my eyes, I roll on my side and curl up in a ball. The spirits will have to find someone else to help them for now. Not going there.

Not yet.

CHAPTER FOUR

THE AFTERNOON SUN peeks through the sheer curtains and tickles my face, warming me. I stretch like my cat Buckley does after his daily siesta on the front-porch swing at home; I reach out my arms, then follow with my legs. I lift myself off the bed and set about unpacking my things and putting them in the oak dresser. T-shirts and shorts, underwear and jammies. Jeans and nice shirts get hung up in the small armoire. In the bathroom, I line my bottles of Clinique on the counter like obedient little moisturizing soldiers.

Then I hear the familiar *bleep-bleep-bleep* of my BlackBerry.

>K! Check in!

>I'm here. U in Chi-town yet?

I tap my foot impatiently while I wait to hear back from Celia. Sure enough, she responds:

>This place rawks!

>Told u

>what up in CA?

>Getting settled

>The Fairmont?

I giggle and move my fingers along the keyboard.

>Not hardly. Cool, tho!!

>Any activity?

>I just got here, C!

>Cute guys?

>1, but he's 13

>LOL!

Celia sends another one before I can type more.

>Gotta bolt. Shower time.

>No prob. Say hey to Chi 4 me

>Hugs!!! ☺

>Luv ya mean it!

I'm about to get all melancholy and shit about Celia being in *my* Chicago when I hear a rattling on the cabin door. I don't have to open it to know what's going on. Although the mountains are in the background, I can see the spirits gathering outside. People from another realm are lining up like they're here for U2 ticket presales. They must sense what's happening here this week—what happens here regularly—and know there are many like me who can connect with them. Again, I shut my eyes and try to block out the pleas for attention. I can't deal with this yet. I want to relax into my new environment, meet my fellow attendees and counselors before delving further into my paranormal explorations. I mean, I'm still fresh off the Sherry Biddison incident, my out-of-body experience, and finding out that I'm adopted. I need to focus on Kendall before I can help anyone else.

The door flies open, and I think for a moment that the ghosts have invaded my personal space. However, it's a very living person in the form of a perky, thin, cutesy blonde with a shaggy chin-level cut and dark, dark brown eyes.

"Oh my God! Is this place gorgy or what?" she says enthusiastically. A large duffle bag falls from her shoulder to the floor, and a mesh backpack hits the floor as well. She's wearing green fatigues cut off at the knee, flip-flops, and a Billabong long-sleeved T-shirt. My intuition, as well as the dark tan on her face and sun-bleached streaks in her golden hair, tells me she's a total surfer chick.

"Hey! I'm Jessica. Jess Spencer, that is. Jessica sounds so formal, you know?"

She stretches out her sun-kissed hand and I shake it. "Kendall Moorehead. I'm so jealous of your tan."

Jess laughs heartily. "Dude, I'm in the water twenty-four/seven. It's going to kill me to be here in the mountains for a week with no waves."

"Where do you live?" I ask with great curiosity as she begins tugging clothes out of her bag and stashing them haphazardly in the bottom dresser drawer.

"Capistrano Beach."

"Where's that?"

"Orange County."

"Ahhhhh." I used to watch *The O.C.* and *Real Housewives of Orange County;* I know it's a pretty chic and rich area.

Jess holds her hand up though. "Before you start judging

me, my mom is a social worker and my dad is a public de-
fender, so we're not your typical Orange County aristocrats."

I smile weakly. "I wasn't judging."

"Sure you were," she says with a wink. "That's okay."

"Well ... maybe a little."

She unpacks in about three seconds and then flings herself
tummy first across the second bed and looks at me. "So, what's
your story, Moorehead?"

I laugh at her directness. I like that, though. She reminds me
a lot of Rebecca. A pang hits me suddenly, thinking of my
friend who I won't see for a week. Becca's gone to Birmingham,
Alabama, to stay with her cousin Camille, who's in college
there. I regale Jess with the who, what, where, when, why, and
how that is Kendall Moorehead. At least, as best as I can explain
it at this point.

"Heavy, man," she says. "That's a crazy way to find out that
you're adopted."

"Tell me about it." I let out a sigh, but it's not due to frustration. Just 'cause. "So, what's your deal, Spencer?"

Jess rolls onto her back and stares up at the ceiling. "I live in
this wicked cool house that my great-grandparents passed
down to my grandparents and they passed down to my parents.
It's across from the beach and it's totally haunted. I guess I've
known it all my life. I can't wait until I'm eighteen and can
move out and be on my own. That's why I use the ocean as my
escape. Out there in the waves, there's nothing but me and the

water. I control my destiny as I ride the crests, you know? Inside my house, things are just . . . weird."

"Tell me about it," I mutter.

She continues. "I see people's auras. I mean, it's like the world is one big frickin' rainbow for me. I can't just look at someone and see normal flesh and clothes. I see this blinding array of colors. I hope this Oliver dude can help me get a grip on this. It's only when I'm on the waves that I don't have this . . . ability, or whatever it is."

"I've tried reading auras," I say, rolling my BlackBerry around in my palm. "But I have to really concentrate to see them."

Jess smirks. "Lucky you. I just don't want to live in a Rainbow Brite world constantly. I need some sort of . . . normalcy in my life."

"I hear that, g'friend," I say with a laugh.

We venture out of the cabin and onto our front porch. A trellis covered in pink roses separates our unit from the one next door. Jess peers through the openings to report on our neighbors.

"Three girls. We should invite them over."

"Why not?" I call out, "Anyone over there?"

After a moment I hear, "Hey, y'all!"

"Come visit," Jess invites.

In a moment or so, the first of our neighbors rounds the corner, followed by the next girl, and then the next. They look very much alike.

"Triplets?" I ask out loud before I realize I've said anything.

"Hey, y'all," the first girl sings out. "I'm Maddie, and these are my sisters, Erin and Harper. We're the Pucketts."

Jess smacks her hands together. "I've never met triplets. How cool is that?"

Erin grimaces. "It has its advantages . . . and disadvantages."

I can see that while there is a significant family resemblance, each girl is unique. Maddie has long dirty blond hair, Erin's is much lighter, and Harper wears her dark blond hair short. They all have the same greenish eyes, though.

"You guys are fraternal, right?"

Harper nods. "Yep. Mom was taking fertility pills to get pregnant, and all of a sudden, there were three of us."

"Instant family," Jess quips.

"Something like that," Harper says.

We swap the hellos and basic greeting information with the sisters. They're all tall and adorable. Total Southern belles. The Pucketts are in the tenth grade and hail from Cleveland— Alabama, not Ohio. Didn't even know there *was* a Cleveland, Alabama. They don't really disclose what their special powers are, and I don't press them for the info. I'm sure I'll find out in due time. After all, that's what we're here for.

"Excuse me?" someone asks from out on the path. "Is this cabin twelve?"

"No, we're fourteen," Jess says.

"Hey, I'm in twelve," Maddie pipes up. "You must be my roomie?"

The girl steps forward. She seems quiet and shy and a bit reserved. Her long black hair is crimped to the middle of her back and a single braid weaves across her forehead and down the left side of her face. She's plump and pretty with large black eyes.

"I guess so," she says with a shrug. "I'm Willowmeana Martin."

"Maddie Puckett. These are my sisters, Erin and Harper. That's Kendall over there, and Jess."

Willowmeana smiles and nods. Quietly, she says, "Hey there . . . nice to meet you."

I can see from her dark facial features that she's of Native American descent. Also, she's sporting a tattoo of a dream catcher on her upper arm. Oh, right—like my mom wouldn't totally shit if I got a tattoo that big! Well . . . a tattoo at all.

"So, why are you here?" Jess asks unabashedly.

Willowmeana seems taken aback some. "You know. The standard stuff."

Jess keeps up her *Tonight Show* interview. "Like what? I read auras. Kendall's psychic. The Pucketts haven't fessed up either. Come on, Willowmeana, we're your friends."

I'm not sure if Jess's open Californianess will go over big with the Alabamians and Willowmeana. I can see that not all of the girls are as eager to talk about their abilities as Jess Spencer is.

"That's okay," I say, putting my hand on Willowmeana's arm. "You can tell us when you're ready."

"No, no, it's all right. I'm just . . . well, this is the first time I've ever been away from home. The first time I've been out of Canada."

"Oooo, you're a foreigner?" Harper says with excitement.

Erin rolls her eyes. "Canada's, like, attached. Get over it."

"Whatever."

"We're all in unfamiliar territory," I say, not just to Willowmeana but to everyone. "That's why we're here. We all have something we need to deal with. And we're hoping that this retreat will give us answers."

Willowmeana bobs her head in agreement. "I live outside of Vancouver with my father, who's the shaman of our tribe. This was a gigantic deal for him to let me come here."

"Same with our mom," Maddie says. "She's wigged out that I'm seeing ghosts."

"And I'm hearing them," Erin adds.

"And I'm feeling all of their emotions," Harper says with a sigh.

"Lucky me," I say. "I'm cursed with all three."

Jess shakes her blond head. "You all got me beat. What about you, Willow? It's okay to call you Willow, right?"

"Sure. No worries." She darts her eyes around at all of us and then swallows hard. "As for me, I see the souls of deceased animals mostly. They talk to me and tell me all the things that man is doing wrong to the planet."

"Heavy," Jess says. "Maybe you're the cure for global warming."

"I don't know," Willowmeana says with a soft laugh.

I glance around at the gathered group. Not exactly a motley crew, but . . . we're different, nonetheless. Or are we? Perhaps our generation is just more open to the world of spirits around us.

I smile at the girls around me. We're all challenged and here for a purpose. However, maybe I'm *not* the weirdest, after all.

Chapter Five

THE AROMA OF GRILLED HOT DOGS, sizzling burgers, and searing chicken permeates the night air as we make our way to the picnic area on the jutting cliff of the Rose Briar Inn.

"I could totally eat a horse," Maddie exclaims.

"Please don't," Willow quips, the first time she's loosened up in the two hours since we met her. "What? The horse is one of my totem animals."

"I don't think she meant it literally," I say to Willow.

In addition to smelling the various meats, I sense that there's corn, coleslaw, baked beans, grilled veggies; enough of a spread to feed a small town. Or maybe just a houseful of psychic kids.

Chris La'Coston is scurrying around, brandishing a long spatula in the air like she's the conductor of the Boston Pops during the Fourth of July concert. She directs her husband, Glenn, to set the tray of condiments and toppings of tomatoes, cheeses, lettuce, and pickles to the left of the hefty bowl of potato salad. Speedy is underfoot, barking and growling simultaneously for a nip of any scrap from the grill. Chris gently nudges him out of her way, to no avail; she finally gives in and drops a piece of chicken to the ground for the pooch. Speedy triumphantly snags the fowl and disappears into the hydrangea bush.

"Glenn, that dog of yours . . ." Chris says.

Glenn laughs heartily. "He just wants to belong."

Chris wipes her hand on her white apron, which reads "I'd Tell You the Recipe, But Then I'd Have to Kill You." I don't need to know the recipe that badly. The long picnic table is set with a red-and-white-checked paper tablecloth, chunky white candles inside clear hurricane lamps, and plastic dinnerware.

And most of all—there are boys!

Okay, okay, I know that I'm still tending to my wounds after losing Jason Tillson, trying to get over the fact that he suddenly had to move to Where God Lost His Shoes, Alaska, with his father, but it doesn't hurt to look. Does it? My heart lurches in betrayal as I take in the eye candy around me. Jason will always be my first love, no matter what, and I'll admit, it's taking some time to get over him, but I have to keep living. I can't be one of those girls who hole up in their rooms pining for the one and only guys they're supposed to be with. Of course, it's not like Jason's dealing with the same missing-me thing, it seems. It looks like he's moved on without me. Or that's the impression he's given me. While I've had an e-mail almost every day from his twin sister, Taylor, I haven't heard jack squat from Jason. No texts. No calls. No IMs. No Facebooking. No Tweeting. Nothing. *Nada.* Zilch and zero. I suppose he's already fallen in love with some Alaskan girl who can catch a sockeye salmon with her bare hands or skin a live moose or something. You know, some chick who doesn't talk to people's dead relatives and pass them into the light—which always freaked him out.

Sigh.

I really need to get over myself.

That's why I'm here, after all. To. Get. Over. Myself.

We girls approach the party, where the boys are all spread out and chatting with one another while chugging down sodas.

Chris waves at us when she sees the pack arrive. "Come on over, girls. There's plenty to eat."

"And plenty to look at," Jess says. Then she glances at me. "What? I'm single. I'm allowed."

"Not me." Maddie holds up her left hand. On her fourth finger is a chunky blue-stoned class ring. "I'm going with William Burns back home."

"Yeah, and he's a babe," Erin adds.

"Whatever," Harper says.

Seems like one Puckett can't speak without the other two chiming in. It's really cute. They are totally connected, what with that triplet-sharing-a-womb thing they've got going. Much like how Jason and Taylor are connected.

One boy loops his legs from around the picnic table and steps forward. He's a big guy and I know in my mind that he's an offensive lineman for his school's football team.

"Hey, y'all, I'm Greg Swanner."

"Hey, Greg," we girls say in unison, like we rehearsed it or something.

"Where do you live?" Harper asks.

He clears his throat. "Elmore, Alabama."

Erin perks up. "We're from Alabama too. Isn't this a small world?"

"I reckon so," Greg says. Harper and Erin both sort of check him out, and he blushes slightly. "This here's Ricky Raney, from Fort Walton, Florida. He's my roommate."

"Hey," Ricky mutters. "Want a Coke?"

"Diet for me," I say, suddenly feeling tongue-tied. I'm getting a *deep* sense of pain from Ricky that I can't put my finger on. My back aches like I've slept on nails for a week straight. Crippling feeling, in fact. But how can that be when he's standing right in front of me? Maybe there's more to it . . . but I should leave well enough alone for now. Sometimes being empathic really sucks because I can't turn it off. I shift my eyes to Harper, the empathic one of the Pucketts, and I can see she's picking up something from Ricky as well. I guess now's not the time to suss out the emotions of our fellow campers. That's for Oliver Bates and his staff to do.

I take the offered cold can and pop the top. A deep gulp of the aspartame-laced liquid does my body good.

"All right now, all of you kids," Chris says. "Let's get you eating. There's plenty of food here. Have seconds and thirds! Don't be shy."

Jess tosses her blond hair. "What, is she fattening us up for the Thanksgiving kill?"

I giggle, although I have no appetite. "Something like that."

Chris's husband, Glenn, mans the grill as we line up in an orderly fashion with our plates in hand. When it's my turn, I take a hot dog on a bun and a small piece of chicken on the side. I glop on mustard, ketchup, and mayo—yes, I eat mayonnaise on my hot dog, *thankyouverymuch*—and pile a small portion of beans and potato salad on my plate as well. When I get to the table, Evan Christian is horking down an ear of roasted corn so fast that kernels are flying everywhere. Kid seriously needs a bib. A kernel hangs from his bottom lip as he turns to talk to me.

"Kendall, did you meet my roommate?"

I try not to be hypnotized by the corn on Evan Christian's mouth and switch my gaze to the guy across the table, thinking this is who he's talking about. The guy is the perfect image of a brooding teen with his long black hair pulled away from his face into a loose ponytail. His dark complexion speaks of a heritage that's along the lines of Willowmeana's. I can tell by his lanky arms as he moves his food around on his plate that this guy is way over six feet tall. I half expect him to turn into a werewolf or something because of the fierceness that's emanating from his skin.

"Carl Fuller," the kid next to Mr. Fierce says. Oh. That's who Evan Christian was referring to. Carl looks like he's about fifteen and he has a mouthful of metal.

"Hey there, Carl. Where are you from?" I ask, trying not to be distracted by the other kid.

"Outside Portland, Oregon. My mom and dad drove me down and then went to Los Angeles to do the whole Hollywood-tourist thing while I'm here."

"That's cool." I turn my attention back to the ponytailed guy. "And you are?"

Without glancing up, the guy says in a deep voice, "I'm Talking Feathers."

"I beg your pardon?"

Evan Christian seems confused and frowns. "I thought you said your name was Josiah Feingold."

Talking Feathers snaps to attention, drawing up to his full height in his seat. "That's the name my adopted parents gave me, but my birth name is Talking Feathers and I've taken it back."

"I'll just call you TF," Evan Christian says.

"I'll just call you EC," Talking Feathers says with a laugh.

"You're adopted?" I ask with my brows raised.

Talking Feathers looks my way. "Yeah, my mother died when I was born. She was part of the Cherokee Nation. I was adopted by a couple in Harbuck, Tennessee, but I've just started to really identify with my Native side."

"I was adopted too."

"I can see that," he says easily.

"Oh, yeah?"

"Don't ask me how. I just . . . *know*."

Curious, I press. "What kind of awakening are you going through?"

He shrugs as if indifferent; however, he answers. "I started having visions of my birth mother talking to me, warning me of bad things to come, and I started telling people about them. No one wants to listen to a kid, though."

I put my fork down on the plate. "What kind of things were you seeing?"

He takes a honking bite of his burger and chews slowly. After he swallows, he says, "Disasters, mainly. There was this massive tornado last year that destroyed a trailer park. I told my friend Alec it was coming and that his family needed to get out, but they stayed. Not only did they lose their home, Alec's grandmother was trapped in rubble for hours and died of heart failure. Then there was this four-car pileup on the interstate that I saw before it happened. If they'da listened to me and closed off the exit like I told 'em, it wouldn't have happened. Of course, the sheriff was all pissed afterward and wanted to know what I had to do with it." Josiah slams his fist onto the table. "Do you know how frustrating it is to see all these horrible things that are going to happen and not be able to do anything about them?"

I let out a sigh. "As a matter of fact, I do."

"I doubt it," he snaps.

Flattening my lips together, I say, "I saw my *own* death. And then experienced it."

"Oh." He lifts his blue eyes. "Sorry. That's heavy."

"Yeah, tell me about it." I think I'll save the whole near-death experience story for another time. Food's getting cold, and reality doesn't go well with grilling outside with new friends.

Just then, a dapper-dressed Sean Combs wannabe plops down to the left of Jess and grins right at her. "You're cute," he says with a huge smile.

Her jaw drops. "Umm, you're forward, aren't you?"

"I calls them as I sees them." His laughter is infectious, and Jess smiles back. "Micah Davidson. I'm a junior from Cary, Illinois," he says.

I nearly bounce in place. "Hey, I'm originally from Chicago!"

Micah reaches his dark hand across the table and fist bumps me. "Tru' dat, homegirl."

The chatter between boys and girls continues as I pick at my food. My appetite isn't very strong right now. I haven't really eaten a whole bunch since my hospitalization a few weeks ago—mostly soup and sandwiches. Mom's worried that I've lost too much weight. Eight pounds isn't a lot, and besides, all the Southern cooking I'd been ingesting was starting to show. Thing is, I don't want to be rude to Chris and Glenn after all their culinary efforts on our behalf, so I start nibbling at the hot dog, cutting bites off with my knife and fork and popping them into my mouth as I listen to the chatter around me.

So, we've got six girls and six guys. That's not a bad mix. I wonder if they planned it that way. I hope they won't be, like, matching us up together or anything in some sort of spring break speed-dating thing. Don't remember the brochure or itinerary including that. Although the guys seem nice enough and friendly. I have to remember that each of them has something he needs help with, just like me. No matter how cute they may be, no one is anywhere in the vicinity of the neighborhood of Jason Tillson. Besides, it's not like I'm looking to replace Jason immediately. I mean, Talking Feathers is cute in an angst-filled way, and Micah's got that whole confident hiphop look down, but I'm not going there. Not with TF. Not with Micah. Not with anyone. I'm here to straighten out my life, not screw it up more.

Tears mist across my eyes and I dare not blink for fear they'll fall down my cheeks and I'll have to explain myself to everyone around me. I'll have to tell the other girls that I'm crying over *a guy* and that I don't know how to move forward with my psychic abilities thanks to an evil, vindictive ghost. Sure, this retreat is for people like me, but we all have our own stories, our own burdens we bring with us, and our own crosses that we must bear.

Chris claps her hands to get our attention. "I know what this party is missing! Music! We should turn the CD player on. Glenn?"

He shouts out, "Tending to the burgers, my love."

Feeling grateful for the distraction, I stand to volunteer. "I'll do it, Mrs. La'Coston."

"How sweet of you, Kendall. The CD player is in the front room. Just click it on and we'll be able to hear it out here."

"Yes, ma'am."

I wipe my hands on the napkin and make my way up the tall wooden staircase on the side of the hill to the main house. Elephant ferns stretch across the path, impeding my progress up the steep steps. Once at the top, I see the headlights of a black sedan that's backing out of the driveway, and I wonder if perhaps Oliver Bates has finally arrived.

A million questions run through my mind over what I should/could/will/won't ask Oliver Bates about handling my gifts and dealing with the spirit world. Questions that will have to wait until the retreat officially starts, in the morning. Right now, my duty is to hit the music switch.

In the front room, I weave through the myriad couches and furniture to the shelf where the stereo sits. I press the power button, and soon the crooning voice of Frank Sinatra fills the air, piping down to the cookout area. I turn to head back to the party and trip on something bulky that sends me flying over the shaggy rug; I land on my arse with a thud.

"Ouch! Damnit!"

Good thing I hit something semi-soft. Three more steps and I would have been on the flagstones, and that wouldn't have been pretty.

"Why don't you watch where you're going?" I hear someone shout.

"Are you kidding me?" I scream, my butt cheeks stinging through the fabric of my Simply Vera jeans. The perpetrator of my trip lies supine on the floor next to a beige armchair. "Who leaves a guitar case in the middle of the—"

It's not just any guitar case but one with familiar stickers. The Beatles, Rolling Stones, the Doors, Jimmy Buffett, Hall and Oates, Bon Jovi, and Nine Inch Nails. How could this have happened twice in the same day?

Someone is in front of me and I gradually lift my head. I follow the length of black sneakered feet up to too-too-tight Levi's and then farther up to a black T-shirt with an electric blue stingray in the middle of it. Up even farther, I see the sun-glassed, knit hatted guy from the airport who chastised me before. I'm about to give him a good piece of my mind when he reaches up and, in one fluid motion, peels off his shades and jerks off his cap.

I'm staring into the eyes I've seen so many times before in my visions, along with that black hair dotted with gray at the temples, even though this guy is no older than I am.

I'm face to face with none other than Hershey Eyes.

CHAPTER SIX

"You!" I say with force.

"You!" he echoes.

So ridonkulous that we both do that you/you thing. Obviously for different reasons, though. Me because it's the living, breathing vision of Hershey Eyes, and him because he's all Mr. Attitude about his frickin' guitar.

"You're that klutz from the airport," he says.

"And you're the idiot who keeps putting his shit on the floor."

He pulls back somewhat in surprise. "Do you have any idea how valuable that ax is?"

I crinkle my brow. "I thought it was a guitar."

He rolls his gorgeous dark chocolate brown eyes and his black eyebrows lift. "An ax *is* a guitar."

"Oh." I stab my fists to my sides, pulling my T-shirt a little too tightly against the girls. "Whatever it is, if it's so important and so valuable, why do you continue to leave it where people can fall over it?"

"I was told someone would be taking my bags to my room."

His lips are moving, but I've ceased hearing what he's saying. My heart slams away in my chest like a demolition crew whacking down a condemned building. I actually dreamed about this guy. Just like I did about Jason Tillson coming into my life. How is that possible? Then I harrumph to myself. Anything's possible when you're a psychic/sensitive/medium/empath. *Hello!* Does this mean that Hershey Eyes and I are going to hook up, like Jason and I did? I don't *think* so. Sure, this guy is a babe in his own right—those eyes with the perfectly formed jet-black eyebrows over them and the absurdly long charcoal eyelashes that have no business being gifted to a guy—but he's rude and is totally Mr. Attitude. Where are his manners? Can't he just apologize and be nice about the whole tripping incident?

He snaps his fingers in front of me. "Hello? Are you even listening?"

"Huh? What? Sorry. What were you saying?"

He shakes his sort of long hair that just reaches the neck of his black T-shirt. "Never mind. So what's the deal here?"

Questions start roller-coastering in my mind, up and down, side to side. "Why did you just now get here?"

"My driver took a detour and ended up on the ninety-nine in massive traffic."

I bite my bottom lip and nod. "Why didn't we just ride in the same car? You know, since we were at the airport at the same time?"

He lifts his arms. "Beats me. Does it really matter?"

"Certainly not. I wouldn't want to be stuck in a car with you for that long of a ride."

He quirks a smile at me. "Ouch. Score one for the pretty brunette."

The flush on my cheeks moves down, gradually consuming my neck and chest. *Why* am I letting this jerk get to me? "So, do you want to, like, join the party or whatever?"

Smoooooooth, Kendall.

"That's why I'm here."

I reach out to help pick up his guitar case, but he tenses. I see now that he's wearing leather gloves, like the ones my dad uses when he plays golf. I don't know whether this is some sort of a fashion trend where Hershey Eyes lives or if he's just waiting for his tee time at the nearest country club.

He notices me staring at his gloved hands and shoves them into the pockets of his jeans. "I'm fine here. You can get back to the party."

Trying not to be offended, I straighten. "Are you coming down?"

"Eventually."

"Okay then." Our eyes lock, and I sense my knees actually going weak, like they're suddenly made of Jell-O. Give me a break! I need to get some distance from Hershey Eyes, so I dash down the stairs and find Jessica and the Pucketts, who are trying to decide who the cutest guy here is.

"Check out the new guy," Maddie says to Erin with a nudge of her elbow.

I don't have to glance over my shoulder to know who it is.

"Who's he?" Harper asks.

"Yum," Jess notes. "Does it matter?"

"Are you all in heat?" Willow comments. "We don't have to go there."

Jess and the Pucketts just snicker.

I pick up my half-eaten hot dog and begin to cram it in my mouth just to have something to do. After I swallow, I concur with Willow. "We don't have to go there."

Jess winks over at the guys and says, "Oh, honey, we're *definitely* going there."

I manage to satiate my sudden appetite with an ear of corn and two fresh-baked chocolate chip cookies. Glenn and Chris have shut down the grill, but they've started a small bonfire in a rock pit over in the clearing. The soft music tints the chilly night air, and I feel myself being drawn to the warmth of the flames. Everyone is making small talk, and people are meeting one another, so I snatch another Diet Coke from the cooler and decide to offer an olive branch to Hershey Eyes.

Even though it's after sundown, he's put his shades back on, blocking off those rich brown orbs from others' view. I go over to the chaises near the fire pit, where he's stretched out, wolfing down his third—yes, I counted—hot dog.

I extend my hand politely and say, "I'm Kendall Moorehead from Radisson, Georgia."

He looks at my hand like it's going to cause him physical pain if he takes it, so I pull it back to my side. Ohhhhh-kay.

"I just thought you should know my name, since you're, like, hating me and such." I add a smile to my snarky comment for good measure.

He lifts his gloved hand and puts the last bite of his hot dog in his mouth. "I'm Patrick Lynn," he mutters with his mouth full. "And I don't necessarily hate you."

Returning my ignored hand to my jean pocket, I lower myself to the chaise next to him. "I don't necessarily hate you either, so we're even."

"Fair enough." He actually follows that with a chuckle.

Time to try and make nice. "So where are you from, Patrick Lynn?"

Chewing the final bite of his hot dog seems to take a few moments, then he says, "I live on MacDill Air Force Base, just a bit south of Tampa."

"Ahh . . . military brat."

"Yep. My whole life. Air Force has been all I've ever known. My dad used to be part of NASA."

"Whoa! Has he gone up on the space shuttle?"

Patrick shakes his head. "Nah . . . he was supposed to, but his mission got scratched because of some horrendous storm or something. He mainly flies a computer terminal nowadays."

Fiddling with the tab of my soda, I say, "That must have been hard on him."

"He dealt with it. Just like he dealt with Mom leaving him. Sticking him with me and my kid brother, Brandon."

I want to reach out to him, but considering that he wouldn't even shake my hand with his gloves on, I figure he's got some sort of skin-to-skin phobia. Instead, I try to empathize. "I'm sorry about your mom. I lost my mom too. Well, my birth mom, that is. She died when she had me."

His head cocks toward me, but I can't see his eyes. "That's got to suck."

"It does. But the family who adopted me is wonderful."

"Well, you're lucky for that."

He toys with his gloves for a moment and then tugs off the right one. I think I'm going to get a makeup shake, but nothing of the sort. He just stares at his hand and taps the leather of the glove over his palm. We sit in silence, sipping our drinks and gazing up at the night sky, while others scurry around us making small talk.

As if on cue, we simultaneously move to place our soda cans on the small table between us. Our fingers touch and . . . *bam!* A spark. A jump. A minuscule moment of contact that could power an electric car. My skin completely tingles where it's touching his, and I try to read him, this quirky Patrick Lynn with the stray grays and protective cover. Suddenly, I know he's not the rude jerk he's pretending to be. There's more to Patrick Lynn. *Much* more. But there's a barrier. A reef of sorts, churning information like rolling waves that slap at me. He's . . blocking me. A wall of energy gushes from him, nearly knocking me back in the chaise with its force. Patrick is trying to cover up something and hide himself from the rest of the group under that knit cap, gloves, and shades.

"Stop," he says firmly, jerking his hand away and plunging it into the safe haven of his leather glove.

"Stop what?" I ask innocently.

"Don't try to read me, Kendall."

"I'm ... I'm ... er ... I wasn't ..."

"Yeah, you were. Leave it alone."

"It's just that—" Oh, well. He busted me. Maybe it's not the nicest thing to try to read someone you just met. "Sorry."

He wets his lips with his tongue and lets out a sigh. "So am I. Believe me. So am I."

Before I can ask what he means by that, Chris rings a loud bell to gather all of us together. Patrick stands. Reluctantly, I stand too and follow Patrick to the group. Jess pats the bench next to her and motions me over with her head. Although I can't actually see Patrick's eyes, I feel them on my back as I make my way through the small group and take a seat.

He's got secrets and questions, of that I'm sure. Hopefully our host for the week can provide the answers for him. I know I can't. It's weird enough that I had visions of him. I can't be his salvation too, and I shouldn't even try.

Chris steps up and speaks loudly to all of us.

"Kids, I'm thrilled to introduce you to the host of your Enlightened Youth Retreat. From television's *Ethereal Evidence*, help me welcome psychic and medium Oliver Bates!"

We break into applause and the outside lamps of the complex click on as bright as airplane lights. At the top of the staircase I just went up and down stands a man in a black suit and a gray-striped shirt. He makes his way down the steps, careful not to trample the elephant ferns like I did. At the bottom, he waves.

"Welcome to all of you!" he says.

I may not be sure of a lot of things, but of this I'm certain: "Oliver Bates is *much* shorter in real life than he is on television," I whisper to Jess.

"Shhhh."

"I'm like five-six on a good day, and I bet I'm taller than him."

She growls, "I said, shhhh."

"That's the illusion of television for you."

"Kendall, would you *be quiet.*"

I stifle my giggle and pay attention. Oliver walks through our crowd of thirteen and shakes everyone's hand. He knows our names on sight. I don't know whether that's because he's psychic or because he read our applications and memorized our information.

Standing in front of me, he smiles kindly and offers me his hand. "Kendall Moorehead. I'm so glad we could fit you in for this week."

"Thanks, Mr. Bates."

"Call me Oliver."

"Okay . . . wow, then—Oliver. I appreciate your having me."

He covers our joined hands with his other one and pats for a second. He's connecting with me somehow, but the transfer of information is one-way. I'm not sure why he's doing this, so I try that blocking thing that Patrick did on me earlier, sending out a mental barrier. Oliver pauses and then smiles at me.

"Very well, Kendall. We'll talk soon." And then he moves on to Jessica.

Did he sense my fear, like dogs can? Probably so. Who knows?

Oliver finishes his handshaking and returns to the bottom of the stairs. "You've all come here for your own reasons. I won't try to pick them apart right now, but there are some of you here blocking your abilities. There are others who don't understand them. Some who doubt. Many who question. And that's what I'm here for. We've got an interesting week ahead of us at the lovely Rose Briar Inn. Chris and Glenn will be taking care of you twenty-four/seven in terms of the hotel, food, and general hospitality. You'll meet the counselors in the morning and they'll be the ones to help you along your path, whether it be to hone your psychic abilities, read auras, dabble with reading tarot or runes, dowsing or divining, healing, whatever you need counseling on. There will be group and individual sessions, group discussions, meditation, and my favorite thing, a very special field trip."

"Where to?" Maddie asks Jess and me.

Oliver shifts his eyes to Maddie. "For now it's a secret, but I will tell you it's very spiritual, emotional, and quite moving. It's where you'll face your biggest fear when it comes to your abilities. What it is that might be holding you back or scaring you. And it's where you'll find additional guidance to help you through it. That's what you're here for. To enlighten yourself. Not until you truly accept the particular gift you've been given will you be able to fully use it to help others."

This certainly isn't something I haven't heard before from Loreen and Father Massimo. But my parents paid good money for me to be here, so I won't block myself anymore and will try to be more open-minded to what Oliver and his staff have in store for us.

This is one of those times that I truly miss Emily. My spirit guide ... my mother. She'd have something smart, comforting, and appropriate to say at this moment. It makes no sense to me how her spirit was with me my whole life, but as soon as I figured out she was there, she left. She passed into the light. Just when I needed her most. I've lost my mother twice. Maybe that's something Oliver can help me accept and move past.

"We all have things we have to accept and move past," I hear next to me.

My head snaps up and I see Patrick right there. His sunglasses are up on his forehead, revealing the deep, dark eyes that seem to go on for miles. Speechless, I feel I could drown in their depths. I chortle in spite of myself and my thoughts.

He jerks to attention and hurriedly tugs his sunglasses into place. "Drowning's no laughing matter, Kendall."

Is he reading my thoughts?

Hot flames paint my cheeks, and the animal instinct part of me chooses flight instead of fight when I see my roommate and the other kids headed toward the cabins.

"Jess! Wait up!" I call out. "See you in the morning, Patrick."

"Bright and early, I'm sure."

Jess loops her arm through mine and drags me in the direction of our cabin. "*What* is up with you and the intense guy?"

"Nothing!" I snap. "Not a damn thing."

Laughter spills out of Jess. "Oh, honey. I'm not a psychic, but even *I* can tell something's going to happen with you two."

My intuition tells me that she's right.

CHAPTER SEVEN

I'M FLOATING AWAY. In clouds, perhaps? No . . . in waves.

Peaceful, lapping water—or is it? Menacing salty fingers grab at me. The churning foam of the ocean pulls and tugs my limbs, drawing me into its depths. Sea foam green that looks so pretty as a wall color but terrifying as a grave marker.

Help me! Help! I call out.

Who can hear me? Who can help me?

Oh no, not again. Not another disaster on the horizon of my life.

Can anyone save me? Can I save myself?

Through the mirrored haze of confusion, I see him. Hershey Eyes. No, he has a real name. Patrick. Patrick Lynn. His eyes are so deep and mysterious that they beckon and call to me even in my darkest hour.

He kisses me. Lips so cool. Attitude to match.

"I've got you, Kendall."

Words I've heard before, only not from him.

The strained buzz from the monitor signaling the end of life. A sound I've heard before. A sound that represented my heart.

Only now my heart cries out for . . .

"Ahhh!"

I bolt straight up in bed. Sweat covers me, imprinting my shape on the pink sheets of cabin 14 at the Rose Briar Inn.

"Kendall?" Jess asks softly from her side of the room. "Are you okay?"

Slowing my rapid breathing, I say, "Yeah. I guess." I tug the black elastic from my wrist and wrench my long hair up into a messy ponytail/bun thing to get it off my moist neck.

"Nightmare?"

"Something like that." Or the most heavenly dream ever of being kissed by Patrick Lynn. Must block that thought before 8:00 a.m. arrives and he can read me over my morning waffles.

"I have vivid dreams too," Jess admits. "I think it's a teenage thing. Rite of passage and all. Especially for kids like us. Our minds are so active when we sleep. We're working out a lot of shit in our subconscious, you know?"

I snicker. "Some rite of passage. Can't I just, like, have to toilet paper someone's house or clean a bathroom with a toothbrush like they do in fraternities and sororities?"

"Nah," she says. "Hazing like that got outlawed years ago. Teenagehood is sheer torture. We just have to deal with it. Sooner or later, we'll be out of it and be adults in the work force trying to pay our mortgage, take out the garbage, feed our kids and get them to Scouts and soccer. We'll worry and stress about bills and pray we won't get laid off from our jobs, all the time wishing we were teenagers again."

She's got a point.

"Go back to sleep, Jess. Sorry."

It's not long before my roommate's soft snore sounds in the room.

I stare at the clock; it reads 1:11 a.m., 4:11 a.m. back home. Sleep does not come quickly . . . or last long.

Before I know it, Ms. Morning Person, Jessica Spencer, is bouncing off the walls like she's had about ten 5-Hour Energy drinks.

"Good mooooorning, Kendall," she sings out. "It's a beautiful day in the mountains with the sun shining and the trees waving to us."

I crack my eyes open. "Are you on some sort of mood-altering medication?"

"Fresh air, baby, fresh air. I've grown up with the smog of the LA area. You've got to give me this."

"Whatever," I say with a snicker. I swing my feet around and drag my East Coast ass out of bed. Jess is already showered, madeup, and dressed to go. I forgo a shower and drag the brush through my unruly, tangled curls. I throw on a woven tank top and my jeans after I brush my teeth and spray a little Secret on. I follow Jess out of the cabin and up to breakfast, wondering what exactly the day will bring.

"What am I smelling?" Harper Puckett asks when we all enter the large kitchen.

Chris is hard at work at the stove, oven mitts covering both her hands. "You kids sit at the table and help yourself to coffee, juice, or whatever."

Evan Christian, Ricky, and Carl all tromp in and join us at the table. I'm so not a coffee drinker, but following last night's lack of slumber, I'm going to need all of the caffeine I can get. I pour the thick black liquid into a mug and dump about five teaspoons of sugar in before topping it off with maybe half a cup of cream. Ahhh ... there, now that nasty, bitter coffee taste is covered up.

"Everyone sleep well?" Chris asks.

A couple of the guys let out grunts and I just sigh.

Chris smiles wide. "Oh, you Easties will adjust. And the mountain air will be amazing for you. Really clears your head."

For now, I'll settle for feeding my stomach.

We all sit at the long table and pass around Chris's culinary creation of sausage-egg-and-cheese bread pudding. It's soft and creamy and exactly what I need to get the day going. Maddie, Erin, and Harper are deep in a discussion about some girl at their high school who e-mailed them about some drama that's going on ... I can't keep up. Evan Christian and Carl are talking about who believes in the Loch Ness monster and/or Bigfoot. Are they serious? Ricky and Greg both seem half asleep, and Micah and Jess are discussing what's on each other's iPods. I shovel in the egg-and-sausage mixture and reach for seconds, wondering where Patrick is this morning.

No, no ... don't think about him.

Willowmeana and Talking Feathers, as reserved as both of them are, have their heads bent together and are chatting quietly. Everyone is already beginning to pair off, even before we've had our first meeting with the counselors. Is this why we came here? To hook up?

Of course, that leads me back to thoughts of Patrick. And memories of my dream.

That kiss felt so real.

Then again, *he's* real.

I need to get him out of my head. I need to get my head in the game. Focus on why I'm here and what I'm doing.

"So who's rooming with the dude in the sunglasses?" Erin asks.

None of the guys respond.

"He's odd man out," Greg says. "Must be sleepin' on the porch."

Chris moves around the table to refill coffee and orange juice. "Now, now, be nice," she says. "His name is Patrick Lynn and the boy has had a traumatic experience and has to have his own room. Oliver usually only takes twelve kids, but he made an exception for him. He's here for help just like all of you, so have some sympathy."

Greg grimaces as he moves the remainder of his breakfast around. "Sorry. Didn't mean no harm."

Chris pats him on the head and then refills his juice glass.

Innnnnnteresting . . .

A traumatic experience? Wonder what that's all about.

You don't need to know, Kendall.

Whoa. Hold the fort. Who just . . .

Emily?

No response.

Is Emily back? It has to be her. Or is it one of the spirits I've felt around this place, spinning and motioning to get my attention? Now they've resorted to bothering me in my head? I do my best to concentrate and block out this invader.

I don't want to deal with any spirits right now, I say inside my head.

Who said I'm a spirit?

My mouth falls open, and I glance about the room. Everyone's either chatting or eating, but that doesn't mean they can't be playing—literal—mind games with me.

Please leave me alone.

Then you do the same for me.

I will, but who is this?

Silence.

Good. Maybe whoever it is is leaving me alone now.

I gather my dishes and take them over to the sink, where Chris thanks me. Others do the same and then we all file downstairs into the massive finished-basement conference room. Wall-to-wall carpet covers the floor, and a humongous, businesslike mahogany table stands in the middle of the room. Gold-trimmed, kingly high-backed chairs covered in red leather circle the table, like we're knights in King Arthur's court. From the looks of this place, good old Oliver must make a pretty penny doing *Ethereal Evidence.*

Now Oliver himself steps into the room wearing designer jeans and a crisp blue button-down shirt. "Why doesn't everyone take a seat and we'll get started?"

The Pucketts take the left side of the table, so Jess and I follow them. Willow tosses a sidelong glance at Josiah "Talking Feathers" and then moves to sit next to him on the other side. When everyone is in place, the seat next to me is available.

Of course, Patrick Lynn saunters in at just that moment and takes the empty chair. I try not to check him out, but it's hard since he's so . . . close. He smells like fresh Dial soap and a spicy deodorant. I really shouldn't be cataloging his smells. Not appropriate. Instead, I watch him in my peripheral vision. A black knit cap adorns his head, but his thick hair shows underneath. He's wearing a T-shirt that reads Got Ghosts?, and it's tucked into a pair of black jeans. The same gloves and sunglasses are in place. Honestly, who does he think he is? Some Hollywood star trying not to be recognized?

"Exactly," he says in a whisper.

I smack him hard on the arm. "Quit doing that."

Jess catches this play and eyeballs me. I roll mine back at her and brush off the interaction.

"So, too good to eat breakfast with the rest of us?" I tease.

Patrick fiddles with the strap on his left glove. "I ate in my room."

"Wow, must be nice. A cabin to yourself and room service."

His face turns to me. "How did you know I had my own room?"

"Deductive reasoning and the other guys being paired up. Chris told us they usually only accept twelve kids at a time, but you're an exception. Here I thought I was the exception because I signed up so late, but it looks like you're the special one here. Why is that, Patrick?" I cock my head to the side in a bit of a challenge.

Patrick presses his lips together. "If you must know, Oliver and my dad went to the Air Force Academy together, so he let me come this week, okay?"

Perplexed, I say, "Oliver Bates went to the Air Force Academy?"

"Yeah," Jess chimes in. "He was a mechanical engineer for the first part of his career. Then he was working on an airplane engine and got hit in the head with one of those mini crane things, and he's been psychic ever since. Don't you watch his show?"

"Ummm, not really," I mumble.

"It's on his website too. He's really amazing," Maddie adds.

A few months ago, I didn't know about anything paranormal or abnormal. I knew nothing about TV ghost-hunting shows; I'd never seen programs about psychic kids, college students who fight demons, or people who solve crimes with ethereal evidence. Now, I'm immersed in all of it. Up to my yin yang. And Patrick Lynn is going to make this week a living hell for me with his 'tude.

There must be peace. I offer him my hand. "Can we call a truce?"

His head tilts down to examine my hand, but he doesn't take it.

"What? Are you afraid of girl cooties?" I ask, unable to stop my giggles.

"No," he says tersely. "I just don't . . . touch. Okay?"

Incredulously, I ask, "You don't what?"

"We've got a truce, Kendall. I just can't touch you . . . or anyone, for that matter."

Questions cascade in my mind like falling dominoes, but there's no time to ask any of them. Oliver Bates calls us to order. I swallow the queries down like a lump of oatmeal. Patrick doesn't move, doesn't flinch, doesn't do anything. He just sits there messing with the strap of his glove.

Is that what he's here for? To get help with his . . . lack of touch? Can Bates's counselors help him? Hell, can they help any of us? And where exactly are these people?

No sooner do I ask the question in my head than an adjoining door opens and in walk four adults.

Chapter Eight

I THINK MY HEAD is going to explode from all the information coming at me.

My hand scribbles notes as quickly as the counselors talk to us this Monday morning. Each counselor has a specialty and will be working with us to sharpen whatever abilities we want to develop.

"The point of being enlightened," Oliver states, "is to open yourself to all possibilities before you. Be open-minded about the things the universe is sending your way. Accept the gifts you've been given by your Creator. Use them to help others and to do good, not to manipulate or make money or exploit people."

"Like his TV show doesn't exploit people?" I hear Greg mutter.

Maddie speaks up. "His show helps close cold-case homicides and missing-persons crimes. The families are totally in on it. He doesn't exploit."

"Well, excuuuuuse me," Greg says.

"Shhhhh," Erin spits, like we're back in fifth grade or something.

Oliver pays us no mind and continues. "I'd like to introduce the wonderful souls who are here to help you with your enlightenment this week. I couldn't ask for a better staff to assist you. First off, this is Heidi Harman."

He points to a tee-tiny woman with white blond hair. Big blue eyes sparkle from her round face, and a vibrant smile shines from one corner of her mouth to the other. She's dressed in a white tracksuit and has a lovely stone amulet around her neck.

"Hi, everyone. I'm thrilled that you're here and I can't wait to work with you. My specialty is energy healing and I use many tools to harness the earth's energies to rid people of ailments. I'm going to teach you the meanings of the earth's stones, as well as how to use Reiki and certain breathing techniques. For those of you who want to focus more on attunement, we have sounding forks that I can show you how to use. Mostly," she continues, "I'm here for you in whatever capacity you need me."

Harper raises her hand. "Are you psychic?"

Heidi thinks for a moment. "I believe we're all psychic in a way; it's a matter of whether or not we choose to use or recognize it. My abilities are more toward healing in whatever form or fashion. I'm feeling connections with several of you at this moment."

The petite woman's energy is definitely reaching out to me, and I feel safe, secure, and comfortable in her presence. I look forward to talking to her about the attunement-healing practice I've been doing at Loreen's shop and whether or not it's what I should be concentrating on.

"Thank you, Heidi," Oliver says. "Next, let me introduce you to Peggy Armer."

An older woman with a shining smile steps to the front. She is wearing a zip-up hoodie with a skull and crossbones on the front of it. Her jeans are bell-bottoms, and work boots cover her feet. She looks as if she could go ghost hunting with Celia, Becca, Taylor, and me at any moment. Her long brown hair is straight and parted in the middle, framing her oval face.

"Hello, children," Peggy says. "It's a pleasure to be here with you. I sense so many wonderful thoughts in this room." She glances about and connects with Harper in particular. "Like you, dear, I'm empathic. For those of you who don't know what that means, I can sense and feel what others are feeling. I take on their pain as my own. I also work a lot with remote viewing, automatic writing, and using a dowsing pendulum. There are several of you here that I will become very close with."

Willowmeana asks, "Can you explain what remote viewing and automatic writing are?"

"Certainly, dear," Peggy says. "Remote viewing is a means by which a sensitive—like many of you—may telepathically view a location from a distance. You may not know it, but the U.S. government used remote viewers during the Cold War to see what the Soviets were up to."

"That's crazy!" Willowmeana says.

"Is that something that interests you?"

Nodding, Willowmeana explains. "Once my mother lost her car keys and I concentrated real hard and was able to see where she'd left them at the grocery store. I drew her a map of where I saw them, and sure enough, they were exactly where I said."

Peggy grins. "That's just what I'm talking about. I'd be happy to work with you—or anyone else—on it."

"So what's automatic writing?" Micah asks.

"Automatic writing is a process by which an individual places a pen or pencil to paper and then, without concentrating on what he or she is writing, allows subconscious thoughts to flow through and guide the pen. This is one of the most basic forms of channeling."

"I've done that," Evan Christian says.

"I'll work with you too, dear."

Oliver steps up. "Thank you, Peggy. She's really got some amazing things to share with you folks this week. Now, let me introduce a very special lady: Mary McCay. She was there to guide me when I had my transformation and became a medium. Mary?"

A short, pleasant-looking mom type joins Oliver. "Thank you, Ollie. I won't take too much time right now, but I will be working with you all on telekinetics, psychokinesis, breathing, yoga, centering yourself, seeking the higher self, and generally mother-henning you, because that's what I do best." With that she pretends she's going to pinch Oliver's cheek, but she stops herself.

"And finally," Oliver says, "let me introduce to you a very special man. A holy man. This is Eddie 'Wisdom Walker' Nelson." A heavyset, older Native American man eases forward, wrapped in what appears to be some sort of animal skin. His long black hair is plaited in two braids. He is the real deal. "Wisdom Walker is going to show you how to find your totem animal and spirit guides to help you move onward in developing your abilities."

Eddie "Wisdom Walker" Nelson speaks not a word; rather, he raises his hand over us and waves it around.

"He's blessing us," Willowmeana explains.

And then he leaves the room, as quietly as he entered.

I glance around at my fellow "enlightened" ones, thinking of the gifts that each of us possess. At least the ones I know of. There are some that even my psychic senses aren't able to pick up. Particularly, the talent that one Patrick Lynn has. Without turning my head, I know that he's just sitting there behind his sunglasses taking it all in, not flinching, fidgeting, or showing any emotion.

I know there's more to him than this bitter façade he's got going. Because I've dreamed of him—three separate occasions now—there's got to be a reason we're both here at the same time. There must be an explanation for why I got in at the last minute to the camp of the guy his father has connections to. Loreen tells me constantly that everything happens for a reason and I'm wondering what in the world brought Patrick Lynn and me together.

My heart races at the thought of some sort of cosmic force directing us to the same spot and time on earth. Tingly sensations zap up and down my hand at the memory of his brief touch last night. A zigzag of emotions scatter through me, ranging from the intrigue of meeting a stranger to the excitement and exhilaration of what's to come. Sure, Jason and I are officially broken up, but I have no idea—as psychic as I am—where Patrick Lynn fits in my life. *If* he fits in my life. It really *could* all just be a coincidence.

There are no coincidences . . .

Okay. Who just said that?

And who's this Jason? If you're broken up, quit thinking of him.

I grind my teeth, seething at this invasion of my privacy. *Who* is doing this? I can't tell if the voice is male or female. Is it one of my *chicas* here messing with me? Or is it one of the guys trying to hit on me in some New Age way? It couldn't be Oliver or a counselor, could it? Maybe it's one of the spirits here at the inn. In any case, it's *not* funny and I don't appreciate it.

Whoever you are . . . piss off. There. That should do it.

Such language from such a pretty girl. Tsk-tsk . . .

"Stop it!" I shout, covering my ears at the same time like that might actually help.

Almost immediately, every eye in the room—even Patrick Lynn's behind his aviators—is turned to me. Some stare at me in dismay, others in shock, but most are chuckling at my outburst.

"Sorry, Oliver," I say meekly. "Just, umm, arguing with the, er . . . voices in my head."

Everyone laughs, even me.

Oliver walks over and puts his hands on my shoulders. "Don't worry, Kendall. Only in a roomful of other enlightened ones does that statement make sense. No one here is going to throw a straitjacket on you and lock you up."

I slump in my chair in relief. "That's good to know."

"One other thing," Oliver says. "The drivers and sedans here at Rose Briar are available for you whenever you want. This is your vacation. Your conference. Yes, there's an itinerary and plenty to do and work on with the counselors. However, I'm not holding you prisoner here. If you want to get out in the area and play, be my guest. All you have to do is sign out a sedan and make sure you don't go anywhere alone. That's my only rule. We're two hours from the ocean and an hour from Yosemite. The world is yours to explore, if that's what you wish."

Jess balls up her fist, extending her pinkie and thumb in opposite directions. "Hang ten, beeyotches! Let's hit the waves!"

That's right . . . California, baby! I smack my hand to the table and turn to Patrick, quite naturally. "I've never been to the Pacific Ocean! We should all go swimming. How awesome will that be?"

Patrick pulls back in his seat, almost cringing at my words.

What did I say? How can this be the guy I've been fantasizing about? He doesn't even like me.

Feeling huffy, I say, "I'm sorry if the thought of hanging out at the beach with me—with us—disgusts you."

"It's not you, Kendall. Trust me," Patrick says in a shaky voice.

"What*ever*." I hate using that word, but it so fits right here. Fine. Stay bundled up in your leather and knit while the rest of us enjoy California Dreamin'.

"This retreat is all about you. You get out of it what you put in," Oliver says. "Got it?"

"Got it," several people say in unison, including me.

I notice that Patrick is silent as a church mouse. He tugs off his sunglasses and presses his thumbs against his eyes, rubbing hard. Dude's gonna go blind pressing like that. Or maybe he's trying to erase a vision or memory. His face is so intense, like he's attempting to solve the world's most elaborate logarithm. God knows that would make me go goofy in six different languages.

He takes his hands down and stares right at me with those eyes of his that seem to cut right through me. I'm expecting some sort of retort to my previous "Whatever," but all he does is ogle, unblinking. The gaze is so forceful that I can't pull away from it. I dare not blink for fear of losing this crackling union.

In my mind's eye, I see Patrick and me ... together ... walking ... one minute we're in a heated discussion, the next a heated embrace.

I jump back, reeling from the hallucination. That's what it's got to be. Me going stark raving bonkers. Sweat dots my forehead and my upper lip. Now I blink like there's no tomorrow. Did Patrick see that delusion too?

As precipitously as the image appeared, it vanishes. But the tension hangs in the air, like drying laundry.

Patrick scares the crap out of me when he shoves his sunglasses back in place and mutters, "I knew I shouldn't have taken them off. I can't deal with this." With that, he pushes out of his chair and hightails it up the basement stairs, away from everyone.

"What was *that* all about?" Jess asks.

Even though I'm in a roomful of psychics, I'm not telling her what just happened. "Beats the heck out of me."

I collapse back in my chair and sigh. A long, deep one that has been building in my chest for the last fifteen minutes. I think I'm in for a whole hell of a lot more than enlightenment on this trip.

Oliver continues with the orientation and I berate whatever spirit guides or angels are leading me on right now. I do believe the fates are pulling a dirty trick on me, having me dream about ... *him.*

Squeezing my eyes shut, I try to forget the mental picture I just had of me in Patrick's arms. I try to forget about the chill bumps I get being around him. I try to forget about the zip-pity-zap when our hands touched.

I try to forget about Patrick Lynn . . . period.

Chapter Nine

"That was fan-frickin'-tastic!" Maddie exclaims as we leave the conference room shortly before noon.

I'm still spinning from the war of wills with Patrick—who stayed gone for the rest of the morning. "What? The dowsing demonstration Heidi did?"

"Yes! Did you see how the pendulum moved when she asked it questions? I've never seen anything like that before. Right, Erin?"

Her sister nods profusely. "Oliver said he has some we can buy to try dowsing on our own. You should get one too, Kendall."

I don't want to sound like a Miss Priss know-it-all. "I already have a couple. I use them when I'm ghost hunting."

Harper chimes in, "You go ghost hunting? Doesn't that scare the crap out of you?"

I lift my hand and wave it in the air, trying to be nonchalant. No need to get into the details of my ghostly horrors at this point. "Not any more than, say, having spirits talk to you any time they want to. You guys know how it is."

"I suppose," Erin says. "But purposely going out and *looking* for ghosts? That seems a little wacked."

"It's not," I say in defense of my ghost-hunting group. "We help people who have entities that are ... causing trouble." To say the least.

"Do you do it like all those people on television?" Maddie asks. "Like with computers and meters and thermometers and stuff?"

I nod. "Exactly."

"That sounds like fun!" Maddie exclaims.

Remembering the tumble down Mayor Donn Shy's front staircase thanks to a supernatural push from her resident spirit is anything but fun. The scar on my torso where my spleen was removed is anything but fun. The vivid memory of sitting in heaven with my Grandma Ethel and my cat Smokey—although it was soothing at the time—is anything but fun.

I clear my throat to unclog the anxiety of days past. "It's work. Something you have to take seriously and responsibly."

How can I explain to the triplets, who are just now experiencing their own awakenings, that ghost hunting isn't all fun, games, silliness, and drama, like you see on the reality shows? Ghosts don't perform for cameras and they don't act on command. It's grueling hours reviewing video and listening to voice recordings in the hopes of finding that *one* piece of evidence to help put the case on a solvable track. It can be incredibly boring when nothing happens or when you debunk an alleged haunting. Mostly for me, it's been life-threatening and life-altering.

How do I make clear that although it seems to be my calling, I don't know if I'll be able to go back to regular investigations, sweeping through people's basements and attics in search of something that proves they have a lingering spirit? Besides, I'm unsure of the state of our ghost-hunting team since we've lost Taylor and her photographic skills (and equipment) and Jason as a protector and skeptic.

Everything's so messed up.

"Maybe you can show us how someday, Kendall," Maddie says with a smile. "We'll come to Georgia over the summer and visit."

I offer a grin back. "Maybe so. That would be fun."

The girls move ahead to their cabin, and I slip into mine. I kick off my flip-flops and look for my sneakers. Jess, Willow, TF, and Micah want to go on a nature walk behind the inn after lunch. It's such a gorgeous day with the Dasani blue—what, I can't recycle that term now that Jason's out of my life?—sky and mulchy green mountains.

The hair on the back of my neck prickles, and an icy cold runs down my arms.

My ears buzz as if they're searching for the right radio frequency.

Oh no . . . something's about to happen.

Then I hear it.

Can you help me?

It's the same voice I heard yesterday. Only this time, there's more of a plea to the tone.

Doing my best to block out the droning request, I rummage under my bed to locate my left Nike. I don't want to acknowledge the spirit. Maybe if I ignore the call for assistance, it'll go away. But the voice implores me, this time in a distinctly female voice.

Please help me . . .

Slowly, I push myself off the floor, a sneaker clutched in each hand. The young woman's pain is so forceful and so directed at my empathic nature that I suddenly have tears running down my face without even knowing I am crying. They're not my tears, though. They're hers. Her despair is palpable, and the only human—and humane—thing to do is turn around and face the entity that I know is in the room with me right now.

I catch my breath at the person before me.

She's about my age, from the looks of her. I can't make out her name yet, but I know she was born in May and she likes to go fishing with her grandfather. The petite girl sits at the edge of Jess's bed, beseeching me with her large, doe-like eyes. Her hair is brown, chestnut almost, and a curly, tangled mess. Dirt coats the knees of her jeans, which are torn in several places. The rips are from something vicious and not merely a fashion statement. Tears continue to course from my eyes, matching the ones that are drying on her grimy cheeks.

I cover my face with my hands to block her from view. If I can't see her, she's not really there, right? I honestly don't know if I'm ready for another hyperemotional spirit. I remember Richie from the airplane and the heart-wrenching message I have to deliver to his mourning fiancée when I get home. Can I honestly help all of these people?

Please go away, I beg in my head to the teenage phantasm. *Let me just have this retreat so I can decide what's next for me.*

However, when I lower my hands, the young girl is still before me. Closer now. Standing a foot away, totally in my space.

"Help find me," she begs.

I stretch a trembling hand out to attempt contact with her. The area in front of me is frigidly cold—if Celia were here with her temperature gauge, I'm sure it would register a major drop. I begin seeing clues and images in my mind. First, I see a rainstorm that turns into hail, pounding the pavement. Then the sound of dolphins rings out, an *eeee . . . eee . . . eee. Hail* plus *eeeee.* Her name is Hailey.

Even though her manifestation has brought the room's temp down, I'm sweating like a pig. A droplet of water trickles down my back and into the waistband of my jeans. The connection with Hailey's spirit is strong and totally draining on me like an hour-long Pilates class.

"Help find me," she repeats.

"Help find you what, exactly? That's not really a complete sentence. Have you misplaced something or are you yourself lost?"

"Pleeeeeeeeeeease."

Then Hailey fades away; apparently she lacks the strength to continue showing herself to me. My empathic tears stop; ones of my own replace them. After a moment, I start to laugh, almost hysterically. I sag in exhaustion and crumple into a heap at the foot of my bed. What a loser I am, lying here on the floor of my room boo-hooing my eyes out because of a ghost. Is this what it's come to? Why couldn't Hailey have appeared next door in the Pucketts' cabin? Why did she choose mine? Why do *I* always have to be the responsible one?

I swipe the back of my hand against my cheeks and smear the wetness on my jeans. I cram my feet into my sneakers and then lift off the floor and open the door to rejoin the others, who hopefully haven't ditched me while I was dilly-dallying with Hailey.

But I find Peggy Armer, one of our counselors, standing there in the frame of my french doors. "We all have to be responsible, Kendall."

"How ... wh ... huh?" Oh, right; she's reading my thoughts too. Geesh, privacy anyone? Apparently not around a bunch of freaking psychics. Do I need to wear a helmet or an aluminum foil hat?

Peggy steeples her fingers together. "I'm sorry, Kendall. I just felt a tug in your direction, telling me you might need me."

I push my hair away from my face and blow out a gust of air. "I do need you, Ms. Armer—"

"Peggy, dear."

"Umm, okay, Peggy. I need all of you. I need to know how to help these spirits without hurting or losing a part of myself."

She smiles calmly. "We all possess certain gifts, and the spirits know which ones of us to reach out to. It's the equivalent of a light on inside a house, emanating its warmth to the outside, inviting the spirits to step forward and knock on the window. You can't squelch the lost souls when they call out, Kendall."

"But I don't want to pay attention to them right now. I've spent the last eight months tending to their wants and needs and every cry for assistance, to the detriment of my own well-being." I clutch my hands together over my heart, feel it hammer like a meat tenderizer pounding steak. "I want to do what's right, but can't I just take care of me for a while?"

"It's perfectly natural to feel that way," she says. "You're at this retreat for a reason, though. You have a gift, a talent, and, believe it or not, a calling. If spirits seek you out, you must know that it's a matter of their trust and belief that *you* are the one to solve whatever is haunting them."

Interesting choice of words. The haunting ones are haunted themselves?

"Center your breathing, dear, and just . . . relax. I'm going to send you some Reiki energy while you concentrate. Now shut your eyes. In. Out. In. Out."

Peggy's mellow voice is reassuring and soothing. Obediently, I close my eyes and follow her instructions. Deep breath in. Exhaaaaaaale slowly. Again. Okay. Good. Yes, this is working. Centering is happening. I'm picturing the air filling my lungs to capacity and then slowly trailing out. My heart rate slows to a more normal pace and my muscles start to relax.

"Wow, Peggy, that really—"

I open my eyes, but I'm all alone.

Willowmeana pops her head around the corner. "You coming, Kendall?"

"Umm, yeah, I was just—" I stop the words and scrutinize my surroundings. Peggy's nowhere to be found. She exited my cabin as stealthily as she arrived, obviously to give me my space. Guess that's what makes her a good counselor. "Yeah, let's eat."

That's what I need. Sustenance and a head-clearing nature walk to flush out my thoughts. Too much funk happening today. A girl can only take so much.

The stroll through the wooded path with my new friends—as well as the hot open-face roast turkey sandwich with dressing and cranberry sauce for lunch—did the trick in cleansing my mind and easing my tension. Now I'm back at the inn, sitting downstairs in the library that's annexed to the large conference room. The space is full of dark, rich colors, and the décor of antique Victorian furniture continues. I shift on the gold couch that's pretty to look at but a pain in the keister to sit on. How British women back in the Victorian days sat on something like this for hours wearing yards of clothing, sweating to death, and waiting for some dude to come a-courtin', I don't get. Thank heavens times have changed and you can just hook up—not in a have-sex way, please!—with someone you have a lot in common with or who you're just naturally attracted to.

Oddly enough, my first thought isn't of my former guy, Jason; rather, it's the rugged face of Patrick Lynn that appears in my mind. All right, I'll admit it: even though he's been nothing but a snarky little turd to me, I'm totally attracted to him. Why do I go for the guys who seem to hate me at first? Oy!

The adjoining door opens and Heidi calls to me. "Are you ready for us, Kendall?"

I shake thoughts of Patrick and his cuteness aside and adjust on the uncomfortable sofa. "Yes, ma'am." It's time for my individual evaluation with the counselors.

Oliver, Peggy, Mary, Heidi, and Wisdom Walker file into the room and take the seats around me. Heidi chooses to assume the lotus position on the floor.

Oliver pulls out a file and smiles at me. "Kendall, we're so happy you could be here with us this week. Your parents were quite adamant that you needed this desperately, due to some challenges you've encountered."

"You can certainly say that," I confirm with a harrumph. I'm so tired of talking about this—so tired of hearing myself whine about it—but I know the counselors need the scoop, so I give them the dollar-fifty version of the story: being shoved down a staircase by a bitter old ghost and having an out-of-body experience while the doctor removed my spleen were a couple of the specific challenges I encountered. "So there you have it," I say, collecting my emotions and trying not to be a weepy sap anymore.

He nods. "I understand, Kendall. And yes, we're here for you. All of us. We will help you." He flips through the manila folder on his lap. "I've been reading over your file and the notes that Dr. Ken Kindberg from Atlanta sent along, per your parents' request. You've had, shall we say, a very taxing awakening thus far."

With a sigh, I agree. "That's true."

Heidi's eyes shine at me. "Tell us everything, dear."

For the next forty-five minutes, I fill the counselors in on all that has happened since I moved from Chicago to Radisson, Georgia. The awakening. Making new friends. Forming the ghost-huntress team. Falling in love with Jason. Losing Jason. The cases we've worked on. The successes. The debunking. The fruit loops we've dealt with. Father Mass and his mentorship. Loreen and her guidance. Emily and her position in my life. The out-of-body trip to see Grandma Ethel. Finding out I'm adopted. Trying to get a grip on exactly *who* I am now. And more important, who I'm *supposed* to be. The adults patiently and attentively listen to my tale, nodding in the right places and covering their hearts in others. When I get to the end, I feel the weight of tears behind my eyes again. I can't believe what a cry-frickin'-baby I've become on this trip. Toughen up, Kendall.

"I'm so tired of crying over this," I say. "In the beginning, it was cool and fun and unique and it got me some popularity at school. My ghost-hunting group has done a lot of good, mind you, and we're making a respectable name for ourselves, but now ... I don't know ... the whole near-death experience really messed with me. I'm almost ... fearful of the spirits now. I never know which one is going to be friendly and which one is going to totally muck with me. I'm not a toy for their enjoyment. I need to either get past this ... major malfunction I'm having and continue to develop my so-called gifts or get on some sort of medication to block this shit altogether." I pause at the use of a wirty dord. "Sorry about that."

Oliver's eyes crinkle. "Don't worry, Kendall. You're free to say whatever you like here. We're not going to suppress you in any way, or judge. That's not our job."

My gaze drops to where my hands are twisted together in my lap. "Thanks. I appreciate that."

Tapping a ballpoint pen against his lips, Oliver takes a moment to contemplate my circumstances. "From all you've told us, Kendall, you've been dabbling in a lot of different areas to test out and strengthen your psychic abilities." He puts down the pen and, fingers laced together, leans toward me. "If you want to get past this mogul in your psychic development rather than medicate your ability away, I believe what we need to concentrate on this week is finding a focus for you. Discovering that *thing* that only Kendall Moorehead can do and what will make you the most comfortable when conversing and interacting with the spirit world." Looking to his counselors, Oliver asks, "So, where do we go with Kendall to help her move forward?"

Heidi speaks up. "I would like to work with you on your connection with the tarot. Although you've been doing some aura readings and attunement healings, I'm sensing that your talent doesn't lie so much in those areas. Your energy is quite strong and it sounds like you've already had some success at your friend Loreen's shop with reading cards for people."

Next, Peggy agrees that my energy is very high and spirits call out to me for a reason. She's going to work with me on how I channel a spirit, teach me to take control as much as I can in a situation where the entity uses me to communicate. Wisdom Walker says he'll walk me through connecting with new spirit guides who are out there to assist me now that Emily has passed on to her eternal peace.

The edginess I've been experiencing begins to ebb, and I let out a puff of air to signify my relief. In front of these knowledgeable counselors who are dedicating their time, energies, and efforts to all of us semi-messed-up kids, I'm starting to feel like the old Kendall. The one who didn't tense up every time she heard a strange voice. The one who didn't poise for an attack when a spirit approached.

"It seems we have a plan for you, Kendall," Oliver says. "Does this course of action seem good?"

I bite my lower lip, not knowing what the right answer is. I have to trust that these people have the experience and knowledge to get me on the right path in my life. I can do this. I can get back to where I was. I can focus on God's overall plan for me and how I'm supposed to lend a hand to others. "Sure. I'm willing to try anything, you guys. Giving up on this gift doesn't seem like an option."

Oliver reaches over and takes my hand. "We can't bury our God-given talent. There's a reason behind all of this. You just have to be yourself and be comfortable in your own skin. We've all been through the indecision and the uncertainty. We're here for you, Kendall. Now go relax."

My courage is returning and I'm excited about working with the different counselors. This was the right place to come. See, Mom *did* know best. Honestly, a year ago, I would have laughed my ass off at anyone who told me he was going to a retreat like this, thinking he needed a net thrown over him and the straitjacket donned tightly. However, I'm ever so grateful that these caring, giving people are here to help.

Maybe I *can* lead a normal life.

Don't count on it . . .

Oh, great. There's that intruding voice again.

You think I like that I can hear your thoughts?

Thanks a lot. *Who the hell are you?*

Nothing. No response. I scrunch my brows together and send out powerful thoughts.

Do I need to hang a Do Not Disturb sign in my head?

Again, silence.

Whoever is invading my mental space needs to back off.

The counselors have their heads bent together, comparing notes, so I don't think it's any of them. Besides, they wouldn't do that. I don't think it's Hailey, because it's not the same voice

I heard in my room. Is it another entity that's hanging out here at the Rose Briar Inn?

And why can't I hear its thoughts?

Because I won't allow it . . .

Then I won't let you hear my thoughts either!

With that, I hold my breath and envision myself inside a large, white, protective bubble of light. A gigamonic sphere of energy that surrounds me in a Force type of way. Obi-Wan would be proud. Nothing can penetrate. Not man. Not spirit.

In annoyance, I lift myself off the couch and jerk open the library door. I jump slightly when I see Patrick sitting there, waiting his turn. He's wearing a long-sleeved black T-shirt with Bar Golf written across the front in large, yellow block letters. His headphones are in place, as are his sunglasses, hat, and gloves.

I stop short and ask, "Are you next?"

He tugs the headset off and must have read my lips. "Yeah. How'd it go?"

"Better than I expected," I say. "We've all got a long journey ahead of us and it's just Monday."

He actually smiles at me. "Tell me about it." Whoa. Nice teeth and crinkly laugh lines around the perimeter of his sunglasses. A jittery warmth spreads over my skin, and my palms itch to reach out and touch him. Holy crappity-crap! Where did *that* come from?

Patrick stands tall and makes for the room I just left. However, I stop him with my hand on his sleeve. His head shifts down to look at where I'm touching him, but he doesn't pull away this time. I wish I could see his brown orbs behind those freaking sunglasses.

A pulse of craving tumbled with good old teenage desire deep down in the pit of my stomach roils all the way through my body at the contact with him. There's an unspoken union of sorts, and clearly this boy is hurting significantly. Information on just *what* is troubling him appears as mixed-up puzzle pieces in my mind that I'm powerless to assemble.

There are those who can help him pull his life together.

Observing my hand resting on his sleeve, I think about withdrawing it, but instead I lift my eyes to his face. My heart is beating ten thousand times a minute. I sip confidence into my lungs. "Let them help you, Patrick," I say, almost in a whisper.

He sighs and then chuckles. "They may not be able to, Kendall."

"Sure they can. Maybe I could too."

He carefully lifts my fingers away from his clothes with his leather-covered hand, careful not to make any contact. "Don't try to save me, Kendall. I don't know if anyone can."

Then Patrick brushes past me and disappears behind the library door without a glimpse back.

It's then that I know that I *will*—somehow—save Patrick Lynn.

Chapter Ten

I slept like the dead—no pun intended—last night after crashing hard. I think I've finally adjusted to Wrong Coast time now. Today—Tuesday—has been an information-filled day. Oliver talked to us about the history of psychic abilities; references date back to the biblical Witch of Endor, who gave King Saul insight into the outcome of his dealings with the Philistines. We also talked about the Oracle of Delphi, a priestess who revealed prophecies as she sat in a cavern that may or may not have emitted hallucinogenic gases that gave the Oracle such visions. Of course, there's Nostradamus and his prophecies, but honestly, any obscure quatrain can seem to predict any historic occurrence. That dude has freaked out a lot of people—still does today!

We talked about the "burning times," when people were persecuted for witchcraft or psychic abilities—talk about intolerant societies. I've heard of the Salem witch trials, but according to Heidi, burnings were common throughout Europe and America from the 1500s to the 1700s. Are you kidding me? Two hundred years of killing people just because they had some future knowledge or special abilities?

Oliver spoke about famous psychics that have paved the way, like the Fox sisters, Margaret, Kate, and Leah, who founded the Spiritualism movement. There was also Madame Blavatsky, who founded the Theosophical Society, and Edgar Cayce, who created the Association for Research and Enlightenment, which is still going strong today. Even Oliver's a member. We had a sparked convo about all the television personalities—no disrespect to Oliver and what he does on his show—like Sylvia Browne, John Edward, and Lisa Williams, and are they for real or just hamming it up for the idiot box.

As I lie here on my bed, digesting Chris's homemade chimichanga, refried beans, and Spanish rice, I flip through my notes. Although much of the day felt like the lead-up to my SATs, there was invaluable information given by the counselors. Only by understanding the history and past can we comprehend our skills, talents, and abilities and find a way to use them for the good of all mankind—or womankind, hello!

Jessica spits toothpaste into the sink and rinses out her mouth. "You buy into all of that stuff about how everyone is psychic?" she says as she comes out of the bathroom.

I shrug the best I can from a supine position. "That's what everyone keeps telling me. I guess it's how you define the whole psychic thing."

She reaches for her cutoff jeans, slips into them, pulls them up over her curvy hips, and leaves the top button undone. "I know, but I don't have any knowledge about the future—or the past, for that matter. I can't predict things and I can't connect with your aunt Fanny."

"I don't have an aunt Fanny," I say with a laugh.

She throws one of the pillows from her bed at me. "You know what I mean. You talk to spirits and can, like, tell people things they don't know. I can only read auras."

I sit up and then lean back into the pillows, adding Jess's to the bunch. "That's a psychic talent too, the fact that you can actually see them. It's an enlightened aptitude."

She throws her hands up. "What do I do with it, though? I want to do Pipe in Hawaii and be on the cover of *Surfer* magazine. How does reading auras fit into that?"

"What's Pipe?"

"Banzai Pipeline. It's a surf reef on Ehukai Beach Park in Oahu. The waves are sick and I can't wait until I'm old enough to travel there and attack them."

"Don't people, like, die doing that?"

Jess's eyes grow wide. "It's the deadliest wave in the world. That's what makes it so . . . desirable. You want to conquer it. Be better than it. You want to sail through it like you're tripping on glass, coming out victorious on the other end in a here-I-am-world fist-raised pose!" She stops and drops her head, her golden hair cascading into her face. "Now, since I'm seeing these mucked-up colors, Pipe looks like, well, a pipe dream."

I swing my legs off the bed and face her. "Never give up on your dream, Jess. No matter what it is." Geesh, now I sound like Heidi, Mary, and Peggy. That's sort of the point, though, isn't it? We're all here to counsel one another and learn from the others' growth. "Read my aura."

"Now?" she asks incredulously.

Hands on hips, I shoot back. "You said you see colors all the time, so what are you getting from me?"

Jess lowers herself to her bed and inspects me. Then she laughs and claps her hands. "I don't know a whole lot about the color definitions yet, but, Kendall . . . you are bathed in three colors." She comes over and spreads her hands out around me. "Violet here, which means you're really spiritually attuned. Duh. Then, over here, you're red, red, red. I'm pretty sure that means you've got like this amazing passion for life and for setting goals and accomplishing them." She pauses and does a once-over of me, as if she were assessing the fashionability of my bunny-covered Victoria's Secret pajama bottoms and tank top. "Pink. Pink, pink, pink . . . all over you, here, here, and here." She points to my heart, head, and face.

"What does that mean?"

She raises her perfectly tweezed eyebrows. "You, my friend, are going to be in a new relationship."

"Right. I just made twelve new friends."

Jess swats at me. "That's not what I mean and you know it. I may not be psychic, but your pinkness reeks of a new relationship. Love is in the air."

I stand up and turn to show her the logo on the buttocks of my pajama bottoms. "You're confusing me with a Victoria's Secret brand. See? Pink. It's written on my ass."

Forming a *W* with her two thumbs and forefingers, Jess says, "What*ever*. You asked."

Before I can sit back down to contemplate whether or not this has anything to do with Patrick and that strange zolt of . . . *whatever* . . . that passed between us, there's a banging on our cabin door.

Maddie Puckett bursts in wearing a turquoise bikini that hugs her slim hips like she's a fashion model. "Y'all come get in the hot tub with us! We asked Glenn to turn it on. Come on!"

"I don't know . . ." I begin.

"Oh, get over it, Kendall," Jess says, tugging her jean shorts off and dashing over to the dresser.

"You did bring a swimsuit, didn't you?" Maddie inquires.

"Sure I did." I just think about how white I am. Though I live in the South, I've been hidden in basements and attics and cemeteries and dark buildings, not an ounce of sunlight touching my skin. There was no time to visit the tanning bed to get that pre–spring break base coat so I wouldn't burn when I went to Tybee Island with my friends. "I'm just so . . . white," I admit.

Maddie rolls her eyes. "You should see Harper. Girl glows like she's been swathed in Liquid Paper."

"I heard that," Harper calls from out on the porch. She enters the room and stands behind Maddie with Erin in tow. Yeah, Harper's a very pale chick, so I don't feel as self-conscious.

I move over to the dresser and tug out the hot pink—again with the pink?—bikini I'd bought at Mega-Mart on wicked-cheap sale for Tybee. If there's a new relationship in the air, as Jessica's aura reading implies, I might as well look my best.

"Scoot over, y'all, or else I'll cannonball in," Greg Swanner shouts.

The Pucketts are spread out in the steaming and bubbling Jacuzzi like the points of a perfect equilateral triangle with Jessica, Willow, and me separating them.

"I don't know how many more people we can fit, Gregory," Maddie says flirtatiously.

Doesn't matter though because Greg jumps into the large tub, displacing the water onto the wooden deck surrounding us.

"My hair!" Erin cries out. "It's in a ponytail for a reason, y'all."

"Sorry," Greg says with an evil grin.

Carl, Micah, and Ricky slide in as well, and the pleasurable relaxation of the steaming water is now more like a crowded bowl of alphabet soup.

"Where's Josiah?" Willow asks.

"TF's back in the room meditating," Carl says. "Evan Christian went to bed."

TF? Oh, right, Talking Feathers. I bite my tongue to keep from asking where Patrick is. He hasn't exactly bonded with the other boys, so they may not know or care. More to the point, I don't quite see him as the hot-tubbing kind.

Jess shifts through the water to sit by Micah, and suddenly it seems as if this night is destined to be a pairing-off if someone doesn't stop it. No one wants to, though. I read their thoughts and desires so clearly it's like I'm holding a newspaper with their lives in the headlines. Micah thinks Jess is *a blond bombshell of a cutie* and Jess thinks he's *majorly fine.* Maddie, while boyfriended at home, is clearly flirting with Greg. Erin and Harper are whispered up with Ricky and Carl, and that pretty much leaves Willow and me.

I scoop some foamy water onto my arms and watch as it trickles back into the tub.

"Sooooo . . ." I say, glancing about. Awkward anyone?

Yep. Quite.

Willow shifts in the water, scooting away from Erin and Carl as they giggle next to her. Can't say I blame her. She flattens her lips and lifts herself out of the tub.

"Whoa! Where are you going?" I ask a bit too dramatically.

She slices her eyes around at the ferocious coupling and says, "I think I'll go meditate with Talking Feathers."

Another one bites the dust. No one pays any mind to her as she glops off leaving wet footprints behind. For that matter, no one pays any mind to me sitting here. Great. What am I, chopped liver? No, it's just that I don't fill out the top of my bikini as well as Jessica and the Puckett triplets do. Not that I'm interested in any of these guys.

I let out a long sigh and lay my head back onto the rim of the Jacuzzi. I try to focus on the massaging action of the jets pressed up against my kidneys as they work their aquatic fingers into my skin. I think of the hot tub in my room and consider slipping away quietly to the cabin to enjoy a long whirlpool session on my own.

Yeah, that sounds like the best idea.

I ease out of the water and wrap myself in the large emerald green towel with *Rose Briar Inn* embossed into the fabric. Oh yeah, I'm totally taking this home with me as a memento. No one seems too brokenhearted that I've vacated the tub; they just spread out more to enjoy the bubbly sensation. I tamp down the itch at the back of my throat that tells me I'm odd man out, which is fine. I didn't fly all the way across America to flirt. I shove my feet into my pink (what's with all the pink?) Reefs and walk across the deck with a *thwap thwap thwap* sound, toward the path back to my cabin.

Coming from the distance is the soft strum of an acoustic guitar. There's only one person here with a guitar: Patrick.

I creep silently toward the music, trying not to be discovered. The moonlight bathes the way in front of me, nearly spotlighting Patrick. He's sitting on a wooden bench under a large bent tree; branches swoop down to provide a canopy for him. The plucked notes reverb off the nearby mountain, making the music sound like he's playing with others. Oddly enough, he's free of the regular disguise he's been sporting. The knit hat lies on the bench next to him, as do the leather gloves and sunglasses. His jet-black hair is all mussed up, and his bangs fall over his forehead in a cascade, just reaching his charcoal eyelashes. He's concentrating hard on the instrument resting on his thigh. His large hands move deftly over the six strings; his left one twists and stretches to form the precise chords. A small white pick sits between his full lips, not in his strumming hand.

He removes the pick and begins to sing ever so quietly about loving everything that a particular girl does and how he should have known better than to mess around with her. Ahhh . . . the Beatles. A favorite of his, I can tell from the stickers on his guitar case. I can't help but wonder if the lyrics are intended for me.

He continues to play, oblivious to my presence. I watch as the moonlight dances over his jet-black hair, setting off that handful of grays at each temple. I squash the desire to sidle up next to him and drag my fingers through its thickness.

I jump at the thought of a tryst with the angsted one. My wet flip-flops squeak against the flagstone, and Patrick looks up with eyes blazing.

"What are you doing?" he asks somewhat brusquely.

Not wanting to react to his terseness, I say, "You're really good."

He shifts his eyes to the strings again, bending his head down so I can no longer see his face. "I'm okay. I only just started playing again and need to get my chops back."

"Well, you sound great to me. I can't play anything but the radio." I wait for him to laugh at my stupid joke—actually my dad's joke. Nothing. "Hmm . . . tough audience," I quip and then move toward the bench. Patrick doesn't flinch when I ease down on the other end. "Everyone was in the hot tub. Why didn't you come join us?"

Still strumming, he says, "Water's not really my thing."

"How can water not be your thing?" I press.

"It's just not, okay?"

Unwilling to drop it, I ask, "Then how do you bathe every day?"

He smacks his hand flat on the strings. "I take showers, okay? Would you like to know what kind of soap I use as well?"

"Geesh. Touchy, aren't we?"

He drags a hand through his hair, moving his bangs away momentarily before they return to exactly where they were. "I'm not here to socialize, you know? I'm dealing with a lot of shit."

"We all are, Patrick."

"Yeah, well, being immersed in water isn't something I agreed to do on this retreat. Can't a guy just play his guitar?"

I lift an eyebrow at him. "I suppose so. I was sort of lonely, so that's why I thought I'd come listen."

His eyes shift up to my face and slice over me, not in a judgmental way or anything. A hint of a smile paints his lips and then he continues to sing the Beatles song. I tap my foot along and sing the lyrics in my head, not wanting to disturb him. His voice is deep and melodic and ever so sexy as he sings about a girl he wants to make his. It's almost as if he wants to make *me* his.

My mouth becomes desert dry.

Swallowing requires an act of Congress.

Reality rushes in like a wave into a tidal basin, drowning me in the salty depths of everything that is Patrick Lynn. I don't know squat about him other than he's an Air Force brat, has a thing about water, and plays a pretty mean ax. I have no idea why he's here or why he's sectioned off from the rest of us. Yet I'm drawn to him.

Patrick twists again and his gaze goes straight through me, like an X-ray into my soul. I didn't realize anyone's eyes could be so . . . hypnotic. The rich brown irises show gold flecks out here underneath the moonlight. Or maybe I'm just losing my mind.

He doesn't blink. Neither do I. Who could even move at a moment like this? Does he feel it too? He has to. Something's taking hold of me. Nothing ghostly or evil, not an entity wanting me to channel it. Rather, the swirling sensation encircling me is like the tingly jets from the Jacuzzi. I'm lightheaded from the intense gaze.

My heart stutters in my chest as if I've just been taken off the bypass machine and everything's starting up again on its own. A quiver begins in my fingers and works its way up my bare arms. Chill bumps break out all over me, and they have nothing to do with the mountain breeze that's suddenly whispering. Patrick leans closer, closer, closer. Intrigue of the moment dances about, cloaking me in jittery excitement. Is he going to kiss me?

"Wooohooo, Kendall!" Maddie Puckett shouts from behind me. "Go for it, girlfriend!"

I pull away from Patrick as far as I can. He withdraws as well, and returns to playing his guitar.

My eyebrows drop and I spin to glare at Maddie. She knows immediately that she shouldn't have been all cheeky like that. A mouthed *sorry* is followed by a wave as she trots down the path to her cabin.

A frustrated sigh escapes me. "That was embarrassing."

"Not really," Patrick says. "Nothing happened."

"Yeah, but it was going to," I say defensively.

He plays a blues lick up and down the guitar in a funky manner and then laughs.

He's incorrigible. Most teenage boys are.

I cross my arms over my chest and huff. Why on earth did I dream about this guy? I wonder with such fierceness that the words echo around in my brain.

Why did I dream of you too?

I snap to attention. "What did you just say?"

Without looking at me, he responds, "I didn't say anything."

"Yes, you did!"

Not out loud . . .

My hand flies to my open mouth. *Oh my God! You can hear my thoughts!*

And you can hear mine.

"You're the one who's been messing with me the past couple of days! Encroaching in my personal space, invading my thoughts."

He stops strumming. "It's not like I want to. Shit happens."

"Apparently so. Can you hear everyone else?"

"Nope." Patrick shakes his head. "Just you."

"*Love*-ly." Not. First I had Emily in my head for months and now I've got some *guy* who can hear all of my thoughts?

I can only hear you when you're close.

"Stop that! Seriously."

Patrick chuckles low in his throat. He's totally enjoying this. Then he lurches forward. "I'm *not* enjoying this. Any of this," he says as he spreads his hands wide. "This is a living hell, let me tell you. It's like having a twenty-four/seven reality show that won't shut up!"

Somewhat ashamed of my actions—Patrick's obviously suffering through some sort of awakening and he's not dealing with it well—I say, "I'm sorry."

He shoves his hands back into his gloves and then stands, gripping the neck of the guitar. "Yeah, well, believe me, I'm sorry too."

Erin, Jessica, and Harper choose that moment to run by wrapped in their towels, dripping hot-tub water behind them. "Kendall, we're making s'mores in our room. Come on!" Jess calls.

"Sure thing," I answer. "I'll be right there."

I have no idea what to say to Patrick. One moment we're this close, and now I want to seriously go put that aluminum foil hat on. Instead of saying something inappropriate, I ease off the bench and slowly turn to walk away. But not before Patrick tries to get the last word.

We'll pick this up later.

His words ricochet in my head and I have no choice but to think, *I guess so.*

CHAPTER ELEVEN

"YOU LOOK LIKE CRAP," Jess says to me as we walk up the path to the dining room the next morning.

"Thanks, so do you," I retort. She doesn't really. "Geesh, make a girl feel special, will you?"

Jess wraps her arm around me. "I'm sorry, Kendall. You've, like, got these dark circles under your eyes and you talked in your sleep all night."

"About what?"

"Not really sure what, but who . . ."

I quirk my mouth to the side, waiting.

Jess shades her eyes from the sun. "Something going on with you and Patrick?"

"No!" I say way too quickly.

"Yeah. Right."

I stop in my tracks at the bottom of the staircase. "Ugh! Is it that obvious?"

Her smile is wide and totally cheesy. "I read auras, honey. Told you. You are Pinky McPinkerton any time he's around. Go for it! He's a total babe!"

"Yeah, I know. But he's got problems."

She rolls her eyes and attacks the steps. "Honey, we *all* do. That's why we're here."

She's got a point.

"One day at a time, Jess. It's Wednesday. This retreat will be over before we know it."

"So?"

"So, I don't need . . . complications."

Jess tsk-tsks. "Life is complicated."

"Ours more than others," I shoot back. "I only mean that in four days, we'll all be hopping back on seven-twenty-sevens and flying our separate ways."

"Not me. I was driven up."

Now I roll my eyes at her. "I just got out of a relationship. I'm not looking for a rebound."

"Mmm," she says with a cat's purr in her voice. "Those are the best."

Erin calls out, "Hey, y'all, wait for us!"

She and Harper jog to catch up and we all walk into the dining room in silence. I know Jess has more to say on the Patrick topic, but for now, the call of Chris's breakfast wafting toward me is what's driving everything. However, I nearly fall over when I see Patrick sitting at the end of the long table, sipping a cup of coffee. A stack of buttermilk pancakes is in front of him, slathered in butter and dripping with maple syrup. His hands are covered in leather and his hair is hidden under the knit hat, but his eyes are free of his usual shades. His brown orbs connect with my hazel ones, and there's a slight smile as he raises the cup to his lips.

Okay. Fine. Whatever.

Boldly, I plop down right next to him. Jess takes the seat across from me and nods her approval.

"Here you go, girls," Chris says as she places a steaming hot plate of pancakes in front of Jess and then me. I reach for the carafe and pour the pungent black coffee into a mug then follow it with a long stream of cream.

Jess lifts up the sugar shell that holds packets of sweetener. "Want some Sweet'n Low? It's pink, you know." She winks.

I squint my eyes at her, ignore the pink-new-relationship aura reference, and snatch four sugars. "No, thanks. I like the real thing."

"I hear that."

"God, the bacon smells a-frickin'-mazing," Maddie sings out, ever the morning person. Her sister Harper passes her the platter with the breakfast meats on it and she loads pork onto her plate. "So, what's on the agenda today?"

Chris places a fresh carton of orange juice on the table and straightens. She wipes her hands on her apron and says, "Oliver and the counselors are expecting you in the conference room for morning sessions as soon as you finish eating."

I nab some bacon myself and luxuriate in the crispiness and saltiness of it. Mom always microwaves our bacon—which is just fine—but I can tell that Chris cooked this in the oven until it was just perfect.

I like my bacon this way too, he says in my head.

A long sigh, followed by my fork knocking against my plate draws everyone's attention to me. "Sorry. Butterfingers."

Smooooooth, Kendall.

Trying to keep it subtle, I narrow my eyes in Patrick's direction and laser my thoughts at him. *Stop doing that. It's creepy enough that you can hear my thoughts. Do you have to do it in front of everyone?*

Didn't sleep much, huh?

Thanks to you, no. Not much at all.

Sorry about that.

I snap my head up and look straight at him. Usually his remarks to me are snarky and somewhat defensive. Not now, though. He seems to sincerely feel bad that my slumber suffered because of him. Maybe Oliver can help us sort this out and tell us why this is happening.

I was thinking the same thing, Patrick says.

Of course you were.

I finish my breakfast in six bites and manage to gag down the bitter coffee. How people drink this stuff all day long, I'll never understand. I don't care if it's got some fancy made-up Italian name like venti grande mucho macho latte-a-chino macchiatto or whatever, it's still nassssstay. But it's waking me up, and that's what matters.

Oliver claps his hands excitedly as we all enter the conference room and settle into seats around him. "Good morning, everyone! Hope you're all ready for a wonderful day."

I take the chair to the right of Jess, much to the chagrin of Micah. He sits on her left instead. Man, talk about something going on! And she dares to question me? G'friend's going to hear it when we get back to the cabin tonight. Ha!

Coming from the room next door, Heidi, Mary, Peggy, and Wisdom Walker file in. Sometimes I wonder if Oliver keeps them locked in there; we never see them hanging out around the inn much. They're very serious about their positions as counselors here at Rose Briar.

Once we're all settled, Oliver begins. "I know you've had personal sessions with the counselors for the past couple of days, discussing the challenges you're facing as enlightened youth. Today, I wanted to bring us all together as a group to really discuss what each of you are experiencing and see how we can work as a cohesive unit to try and help each other through whatever roadblocks are in your way." He turns to his left, where Evan Christian is sitting and scribbling in a small notebook. "Evan Christian, let's start with you, buddy."

"Why me?" the boy asks.

Oliver claps him on the back. "Because you're the closest to me."

Evan Christian laughs softly. "I've told Peggy and Mary everything. I don't want everyone here to think I'm a freak."

"We won't think that," Maddie speaks up. "That's why we're all here."

Licking his lips for confidence, Evan Christian begins. "I don't suppose I possess anything incredible. It's not like I'm a superhero or anything." He proceeds to share with the group what he told me our first day here. He knows things he shouldn't. His parents are wigged out about it. Medication seems to be the answer.

Ricky interrupts. "Why is it that adults want to push the pills at us? My family doctor wanted to give me Demerol. That's some potent stuff."

Peggy says supportively, "Tell the group what you've experienced, Richard."

I listen as Ricky details a story about seeing spirits in his room at night. His doors and windows rattle and things fall off shelves at inopportune times. "My parents think I've got something superbad wrong with me. My mom even thought it was because I listened to grunge. That's not it at all. I listen to loud music to block out the voices in my head. Every time a spirit is present, I get this horrible back pain, like nails being driven into me. Seriously, dude, that's not right."

Without turning my head, I slide my eyes over to where Patrick sits restlessly tugging at the inside tag of his right glove. Many times, the music he's listening to in the headphones is cranked so loud, you can hear the bass beat. I suppose he thinks the tunes confuse the spirits, or at least provide him with a natural mute button.

"Peggy, you can address this, if you'd like." Oliver leans back in his chair and crosses his hands behind his head.

"It's a knee-jerk reaction in our society—in most cultures, for that matter—for someone to deem you as crazy if you hear voices in your head. It doesn't stop it from happening, though. Most professionals equate hearing voices with schizophrenia, insanity, or an injury in which there is swelling on the brain that causes images and sounds in our minds. Also, those who possess extreme talents of some sort—highly creative folks— seem to have these experiences more. These voices are vessels of their own creativity," Peggy explains. She walks around the room, motioning with her hands as she speaks. "Do you have highly creative tendencies, Richard?"

"I paint," he says. "Lots. I dream about painting, and all these abstract images come to me in my sleep. So you're saying it could all be part of the same thing?"

"Very possibly," Peggy says, which makes sense. Doesn't explain me, though. I was a whiz with a box of Crayolas when I was younger, but I can't draw, paint, or sketch my way out of a paper bag. I sing with the CD player, but no church choir would ever feature me on Easter Sunday. I guess that rules out the theory for me.

Me too, Patrick sends to me.

What exactly are *you experiencing, Patrick?*

It's not my turn.

Stubborn ass.

I may possibly be the first girl ever to flirt telepathically. Celia will never believe this.

Peggy continues with her counseling. "It's actually more 'normal' to consider that the voices you are hearing *are* those of ghosts or spirits, possibly a deceased family member or friend who feels they have something pertinent to offer you, advice to help you through a particular situation. Was there an event that prompted these voices, Richard?"

Ricky hangs his head. "Yeah. My grandpa got killed in a drunk-driving accident. He wasn't, like, drunk. The buzzed guy hit him and lived through it."

"Most drunk drivers do survive," Oliver notes.

"This could be your grandpa's way of sending spirit guides to you, to give you guidance in life. It's what we call a paranormal event, and you'll notice that more and more people are coming forward with experiences like this."

"As evidenced by our appearance here at this table," Willow says.

"Exactly, Willowmeana," Peggy says. "Another possible theory is you've been blessed with a spirit guide—not some random spirit, but one who is attached to you for a special reason."

"Who's Emily?" Oliver asks. He twists at his 'stache and he seems to be receiving information. "I'm getting an Emily. Someone's mother. She's been with you your whole life, only you just recently became aware of her."

I know Patrick's next thought before he sends it. *Don't you think you need to fess up, Kendall?*

Slowly, I raise my hand. "Emily was my birth mother."

"Damn, he's good," Jessica hisses.

"Tell us about her, Kendall."

I place my hands on top of the conference table and shrug. "I don't have much to go on. I moved from a very large, loud city to the middle of nowhere. In the silence of my room, a woman appeared to me, talked to me, and made me aware that I could know things psychically. Later, through a vision, I found out she'd been in a car accident and was taken to the hospital; she died shortly after giving birth to me. My mother was her nurse, and she adopted me." This isn't a new story to me, of course, but the people in the room seem rapt. Even Patrick.

That had to be hard for you, Kendall.

No shit, Sherlock.

He and I both snicker at the same time, a shared intimate moment.

Oliver may have picked up on Patrick's and my connection, but he's too busy with the energies swirling around him to say anything. Heidi interjects, "Emily's not with you anymore?"

"No, ma'am," I say. "She passed into the light after I found out the truth. Which totally makes no sense to me! She left me just when I needed her most in my life."

Oliver's head falls back and he twitches in his chair. "She's with me. At least, residual energy from her is. Emily . . . young . . . beautiful. Long, flowing hair." His eyes remain closed; he continues to jerk around. Celia told me he does this a lot on his television show when he's connecting with a spirit. Thank God I don't do that. I'd look ridonkulous. "She wants me to tell you something, Kendall."

"Ohhh-kay." I bite my bottom lip to keep it from trembling. Tears will surely be threatening soon. There are so many things I never got to ask Emily. Who's my father? What about my grandparents? Where was she going when she got in that wreck?

"The answers you seek have nothing to do with Emily," Oliver says, eyes moving underneath his lids like he's in REM sleep. "She says that you 'must find them.'"

"Who? Her parents? My father?"

Oliver vehemently objects with a strident shake of his head. "No, Kendall. It's not about her. It's not about you. It's about *them*. She says you must find them. That's what your ability is for."

Frustration boils in my chest like a case of pneumonia. My thoughts and breath collide in a highway of aggravation and confusion. Who is *them?* Why is everything a puzzle, riddle, or word problem to dissect and solve? It's hard enough being a teenager without this additional crap being thrown at me. My head aches, and nausea begins its trek up from my stomach to my throat. I want to lie down. And just . . . be.

Heidi picks up on my irritation and spreads her hands to send me Reiki energy. I appreciate it, but it's totally not going to work. Not right now.

Are you okay? Patrick implores, sending a surge of energy toward me.

I can't be here right now.

And with that, I push my chair back, stand, and exit the conference room.

Chapter Twelve

In my room, I pace around trying to decipher the message from beyond. This is more complicated than *The Da Vinci Code*. Where's Robert Langdon when *I* need him?

I power up my laptop and wait as it scans the inn's network looking for an open WiFi hot spot. Before my computer is finished with its boot, the familiar ring of my Skype account sounds. For a fleeting moment, I think it might be Jason reaching out from Alaska, but I know better than that. He's moved on. And apparently I have as well.

I'm right; it's not him. But it's someone I need to talk to. The video call indicator pops up, and Celia's avatar shows on the screen—it's a picture of her in that butt-ugly ghost-hunting vest of hers filled with all her equipment.

"Yo, yo, yo, K-dog! What up?" the voice calls out when I press Answer. Slowly, the fuzzy video picture comes into view, and I see a familiar dark-haired person smiling into the camera sporting a brand-new Chicago Cubs baseball cap.

"Celia! You've gone to the dark side," I say with a laugh as my own video box pops up in the lower left-hand corner. "You know I'm a White Sox fan. What's with the treachery?"

She lifts her hand to the blue cap and tips the bill at me. "They were two for one on clearance. Dad's got the White Sox one. What? I'm stylin' in it."

"Whatev," I say with a laugh. It's good to ground myself in the reality of home, even though Celia's not in Radisson. But Chicago's home too. Always will be. I'll forever identify myself with the Windy City. "How's the vacay going?"

Celia's eyes widen. "Oh my God, Kendall. This place is freaktastic! I totally want to move here."

"Don't even think of leaving me before commencement ceremonies are over."

"I have never eaten so much food in my entire life. This is the best beef in the world." The computer screen goes all scrambly and wobbly. "Check out this view," she says. The built-in camera on her laptop is clearly pressed against the glass of her room at the Fairmont. In the distance, I see the sun shining brightly over Lake Michigan with a hint of Navy Pier off to the left. I wish I could sniff the smell of the water.

"I told you it was awesome there."

Celia flops back in front of the computer and peers into the monitor. "I have sooooo much to tell you, but first things first. Are you getting enlightened? What's going on? Is Oliver Bates as cool in person as he seems on television?"

"Whoa there, Nichols. One question at a time." I laugh with

my friend and adjust myself on my bed with the laptop in front of me. "Yes, there's enlightenment out the ass here. We're up to our ears in enlightenment. Lots of sessions with the counselors and the group and learning that I'm not the only screwed-up kid in America. It seems it's running rampant these days."

"How so?"

"Oliver said that since Nine/Eleven, this sort of veil has been lifted around mankind. That people are more open to . . . possibilities and explanations from the other side. There are a lot of questions and not a lot of answers. People want to know where they go—after, you know? So, a psychic kid or one who talks to spirits isn't as freaky-weird as it was when our parents were growing up and stuff."

Nodding, Celia says, "I can buy that. Death isn't merely a physical or religious matter. It's quite scientific, in fact. In science there is one basic, and that's that matter cannot be destroyed. It simply changes its form. So, when we die, the body might be destroyed by bacteria and other microorganisms that are in the soil that feed on the dead. They use some of the bacteria on themselves and others go into the ground to fertilize. The plants then feed on the soil, the animals feed on the plants, the animals are eaten by other animals or man, so we're really all just part of earth's recycling and—"

"Jesus in the garden, Celia! Don't get all biological on my ass. I'll never eat a steak again if you do that."

She laughs heartily. "I'm just saying, Kendall. There are a lot of possibilities."

"That's what we've been talking about."

She squirms around, causing her video feed to break up and sputter. Something's up with her, I can tell.

"What is it you have to tell me?"

"No, no . . . first your camp experience," she insists.

"Celia. It's me. I'm psychic. I know you have something so big that you're about to pee your pants to tell me."

"Actually," she says, "I do have to go to the bathroom. BRB."

I shake my head at no one as the video moves to show the bedspread and a picture hanging above her bed of a sailboat on a lake. Why do hotels have the stupidest, most nonsensical artwork? I guess it's 'cause they get it for cheap.

I hear the toilet flush, the water run, and Celia pound back into the room. The screen bounces as she returns to the bed and adjusts the camera to give me a view up her nostrils.

"That's attractive . . . not!"

"Wait, I've got to—"

"Celia Nichols, if you don't tell me what you're bursting to tell me this instant, I'm going to go insane. And believe me, I'm not far from that mountain cliff."

"Keep your shorts on," she says with a laugh. Then her face grows sober as her eyebrows knit together. "Okay. This is, like, serious. I've been doing a lot of research here while the parentals have been off at this retailer thing. Can you believe they actually hired a limo to drive me around the city and stuff so I'll be safe?"

I press my lips together and fail to mention the limo that brought me from Fresno to the inn. "So—what have you found?"

"You know how you had that vision of a Wisconsin license plate? Well, my cousin Paul, the agent with the Georgia division of the FBI, got the address that the plate was registered to in St. Germain, Wisconsin."

"This is old news, Celia."

"Just wait. Remember the names you had in a vision? John Thomas and Anna Wynn Faulkner? Turns out, that was *their* address, like, twelve years ago!"

My hand flies to my mouth and I nearly gag on the intake of breath. "Emily's parents?" My grandparents?

"Maybe so. They filed a missing-persons report for Emily, so it could very well be the same family, provided that your vision was accurate."

"Oh my gosh, Celia, what if—"

"There's more!" I hear her shuffling through some papers. "They left St. Germain, but there was a connection here in Chicago, which could explain why Emily was here the night she had you and died."

A twinge of sadness shudders through my system as I think about how poor Emily—poor Mom—suffered in the horrible car crash that rainy night. At least they got her to the hospital in time for me to be born. I swallow the chunk of emotions stuck at the back of my throat. "What's the connection?" I manage to get out.

"Stay with me, K," Celia instructs. She knows me so well. "It seems that in addition to the lake house in St. Germain, Wisconsin, John Thomas and Anna Wynn Faulkner had a home in"—she glances down at her notes—"Naperville, Illinois. A suburb of the city."

"Sure. A girl at the coffeehouse where I used to work lived there."

Celia glares at the computer screen like she's going to come through and smack me. "Who cares about some chick who makes java? Listen to me. I got the address in Naperville."

The inflammation in my throat returns. Not sure if it's anticipation or trepidation. "And?"

"Dude, this house. You should see it. It was massive."

I lean into the computer. "You went there?"

"Umm, duh. Charlie the limo driver took me there and waited while I talked to the owners."

"Were they . . . Emily's parents?"

Celia drops her head and all I can see is the Chicago Cubs logo on her hat. Her voice is a little muffled as she reads off her notes. "No, they sold the house two years ago to the Yardley family. They told the Yardleys that they were selling everything, taking out some of John Thomas's savings, and going to see the country in an RV. Of course, that was two years ago, K."

My hands quake at the thought of being so close to my grandparents. They're out there somewhere . . . traveling down the same highway I took to this inn, possibly. I sharpen my psychic eye and look deeply into myself, using everything inside me to determine where these people might be. I see an older man with a mop of white hair, a hearing aid in his left ear, and silver wire glasses. The woman with him is petite, and stylish with her short salt-and-pepper hair. Her smile is bright, and her lipstick is perfect; she sips sparkling water through a straw. Where are they? Where? I grunt slightly, as if I'm forcing the information to just pop up like a Wikipedia page and tell me the answers to all of my questions.

The only thing I pick up, though, is a pair of blue booklets. Blue booklets? Gold lettering. Something small that fits in a pants pocket or a handbag.

"Kendall, you're wigging me out," Celia calls through the computer.

Snapping back, I say, "I was just trying to reach out to their energies. They have to be older now. Older than my parents and yours. Like gray-hair-they've-stopped-dyeing older."

"Are they still alive?" she asks pragmatically. "Sorry, but it's a legit question."

I know it is, so I close my eyes and send my energies out again. Yes. They're very much alive. John Thomas had a bout with prostate cancer last year, and Anna Wynn still sneaks a cigarette on the side every now and then, but they are most definitely alive and . . . somewhere.

"I think I see them, Cel. Do you know what a blue book with gold writing could be?"

Celia crooks her mouth. "You mean like a passport?"

"I don't know. I've never had a passport," I shoot back.

She rummages through her backpack and tugs out a tattered blue booklet with the seal of the United States of America in the middle and the word PASSPORT in large, gold block letters. "Like this?"

"That's it! They had passports in my vision."

"A short trip or expatriates?"

"I don't have the answer."

"Some psychic you are," she jokes.

I try to laugh with her, but my psychic headache begins to ping away at my temples, making me wish I'd packed the big bottle of Motrin for my trip. I squeeze my eyes shut against the pain, trying to will away the pounding. Too much to take in all at once, more than likely.

To Celia, I ask, "Is there any way to cross-reference State Department records to see if they've traveled abroad?"

"I suppose so," she says. "That's asking a lot, considering how tight Homeland Security is on their info these days. Let me get Paul on it."

I breathe out in increments until my lungs feel empty. "Please do that. I need to make sure we're on the right path."

"You got it!" Then Celia adds, "Oh, one more thing. I'm checking on that other name you envisioned. Andy Caminiti?"

"Right."

"Paul's doing a search on him, missing persons, disappearances, arrest records, all of it. I'll let you know what I find out."

Celia's beaming face conveys that she's not doing this only because she's my friend but because she genuinely wants to help and enjoys the investigative nature of this mystery. It's not just any mystery, though. It's my life.

"Thanks for everything, Cel. I don't know what I'd do without you."

She gives me a toothy grin. "You'll never have to worry about that. I'm not going anywhere." There's a sudden silence between us, and I know we're both thinking about the Tillsons. Knowing what she's going to say before the words leave her mouth isn't always fun.

"Have you, like, heard from Jason?" she asks tentatively.

"Not a word." Now's not the time to tell her about Patrick Lynn. She'd just have Paul do some sort of background check on him and his family to see what his story is. I'd rather Patrick tell me when he's ready since I can't read a thing about him. Oh, sure, I can hear his thoughts and he can hear mine, but I don't have the first clue about what other abilities he possesses or how he got them. In due time, he'll tell me. Of that I'm positive.

"I got a text from Taylor," Celia reports. "She's been working on her photography and really building up her portfolio. Her dad took her up to his park on the teeny-tiny seaplane and she said she saw polar bears, bald eagles, a blue whale, a humpback one, a pack of orcas, gray wolves, grizzly bears, a lynx, and three moose."

"Damn. I can't exactly see our little Tay-Tay getting all back to nature, but more power to her."

"She also said Jason's learning to fly. Can you imagine that?"

An image of Jason somewhere in the future, in uniform, flying a large aircraft, crosses my vision. "I can totally believe it."

Celia tugs off her hat and fluffs her messy hair with her hand. "Mom and Dad'll be back soon. Gotta hop in the shower and get ready to go out. I'll keep you posted, K. Just have a good time there and don't worry about a thing."

Easier said than done. "Have you just met me, Cel?"

"Sort of," she says with a laugh. "TTYL!"

"Love ya; mean it," I say, and then click off the window.

I sit in stunned silence for a moment as I let the convo with my best friend sink in. Could Celia have actually found my grandparents' last two addresses? Where are they now? Where did they go? They couldn't have just vanished off the face of the earth. Centering my thoughts, I repeat their names over and over in my head.

John Thomas Faulkner
Anna Wynn Faulkner
John Thomas Faulkner
Anna Wynn Faulkner
Talk to me . . .

Soon, an image of a man and woman surrounded by a dry ice–like substance swirls in my cerebral hemisphere. I breathe in. I breathe out. Concentrating hard to read the details of what I see in my mind's eye. Like static in the air during a lightning storm, a touch of melancholy and sadness surrounds them. A negative attitude about something taken from them.

Well, durr ... that's probably Emily. I only wish I could look at a map and automatically know where they are now. Why isn't that a feature of Google Earth? It doesn't work like that, though. Being psychic doesn't mean I'm omniscient, no matter how hard I deliberate. I squint my closed eyes, like that's going to do any good. I seek out any detail I can relay to Celia, much like I did with the Wisconsin license plate that set us on this journey to begin with.

No matter how hard I strain to see around the two people, it's utterly blocked to me. It's like I need an extra booster rocket to get through the hazy barrier. I blow out my frustration and open my eyes. It's clearly not up to me to solve this mystery. If it were, the answers would come to me more simply. Right? I can just hear Loreen telling me that everything happens for a reason and I can't question God's will. Well, yeah, I'm sorry, but I sort of can on this matter.

A rumble overhead that sounds like the makings of a thunderstorm gets me to sit up and take notice. "Sorry," I yell up to the ceiling, then bite my bottom lip.

Okay, who am I to fight the Almighty? I'll let Celia continue her information quest. She's doing a great job so far and I know she's got my best interests at heart.

Now that I'm over my little freak-out/slight temper tantrum from before, I guess I should return to the conference room and see what's going on. Mom and Dad paid good money for me to be here at this retreat. Moreover, I still want to find out what everyone else's "problem" is, so to speak.

Knowing my luck, I missed Patrick's soulful confession of what powers he possesses and how he got them. Particularly, how he's able to invade my thoughts. I'm sure it's a story for the books.

As my mind swirls in a hundred gazillion directions, I make my way out of the cabin and onto the path. I pause for a moment and then walk over to the bench where Patrick and I sat last night. Where we . . . bonded. (Is that what us kids are calling it these days?) Where our connection was more . . . it was psychic, it was physical, yet not. Was it cosmic or kismet?

I lower my weight onto the slats of the weathered wood, almost experiencing every thunderclap, rain shower, and snowstorm that ever touched this lumber. The scent of pine trees is heavy in the air as the cones are in full bloom for the spring season. I smother a sneeze tickling the roof of my mouth and concentrate on the forest ahead of me and on the remarkable mountain range stretching out over the horizon.

Suddenly, it's like an intuition is tapping me on the shoulder, and I sense that I'm not alone. I hope in vain that it's Patrick coming out to sit with me again, but before I turn to face my companion, I know from the chill in the March air that the person present is not of the living.

Bravely, I find my voice. "Wh-what are you doing here, Hailey?"

Chapter Thirteen

THE YOUNG WOMAN lifts her eyes to my face. "I'm waiting to be found."

"What does that mean?"

"Please help me," she begs.

I shove my hands into my hair and rub at my scalp. "Help you what? Stop talking to me in riddles! If you want help, then talk to me."

She stares at me with her wide, sad eyes. I have to remember that spirits are delicate souls somewhere on a transitional plane. And they were people too, after all. I need to be more sensitive. I gather my thoughts, take a deep breath, and ask, "Where are you? Did you die here at the inn? Is that why you're here?"

She seems perplexed. "I'm here because of you. *You're* supposed to find me. They said you would."

I am? Is this the "they" that Oliver relayed to me? The "find them" that Emily was referring to? Is this some sort of calling that Emily is directing me to through this retreat? My heart is heavy with love and loss and loyalty to the woman who gave me life while losing her own.

"Did someone named Emily say I'd assist you?"

"I don't know their names," Hailey explains. "There were a bunch of them and they said you were the one. Are you or not?"

Gulp. I suppose I am.

For the sake of Emily, a woman missing forever to her family and to the baby she'd never had a real relationship with, I rotate to survey Hailey. Her eyes are even sadder than before, and somehow, it's up to me to fix all that ails her.

I don't know if I can.

I don't know if I want to.

I don't know if I'm capable anymore.

My eyes flutter shut; I'm trying to block Hailey from my mind. Her face still appears on the insides of my lids, though. Loreen's voice is strong in my head, telling me God has given me the skill to reach the deceased because they need my help. Emily told Oliver Bates that there's more for me to do, but part of me wants Mom's boss to prescribe me a big old colorful pill with lots of milligrams that erases this "talent" from my mental hard drive.

Suddenly, Celia's in my thoughts, particularly something she wrote on one of my get-well cards when I was in the hospital. Of course it was encouraging, and from the pen of the Bard himself. In *Richard III,* the king calls out, "O coward conscience, how dost thou afflict me!"

Slamming my fists to the bench, I swallow down the heartburn-y taste of apprehension. Kendall Moorehead may be a

lot of things, but she's not a chicken, faint heart, fraidy cat, jel-
lyfish, lily liver, malingerer, quitter, scaredy-cat, or yellow-bellied
anything. Geesh, there I go, speaking of myself in the third person again. D'oh!

Hailey is not here to injure me in any way. She honestly
needs my aid, and I will give it to her. I scan her thoughts and
I'm assured that she doesn't mean to harm me, like Sherry
Biddison did. Not all spirits are like Sherry Biddison. There is no
hatred in Hailey's heart. Nor does she want to push me down
the side of this mountain or anything. I have to have faith. In my
God. In my abilities. In Hailey's outreach to me.

It has to be this way.

"Find me, please," she says in a ghost of a whisper.

I'm ready to intercede on Hailey's behalf any way I can. This
is my calling. It's what my mother wants me to do. I reach out
to Hailey and say, "Tell me everything you know."

I've seen reruns of the old, old *Star Trek* episodes where that
pointy-eared Spock guy mind-melds with people so he can
read their thoughts and memories. He'd place his fingers strate-
gically on the person's forehead and sinuses, and all of a sudden,
Spock would, like, have the privilege of total knowledge. It
looks so frickin' easy on television—then again, it's television.
This is real life and I'm doing my best to connect on some sort
of telepathic level with Hailey. She sits patiently next to me because she knows now that I will do everything I can to facilitate
people finding her.

But my energy spark is off. I'm having one hell of a time bonding, no matter how hard I concentrate. I hold my breath, but that does no good. I strain, my muscles seriously burning . . . nothing. I don't know what's wrong. I've never had trouble seeing a spirit's past or what they need from me when they specifically seek me out. Maybe it's all the stress and anxiety of this retreat and wanting to fit in with the other kids.

"Can I help you, sweetie?" I hear behind me.

Coming down the path is one of the counselors. She's on the lookout for me, like I've sent some sort of beacon of need out to the universe. Hmmm . . . maybe I did and didn't even know it.

There stands Heidi, all tiny and sweet with her kind eyes and her hands spread out, palms up. "You need a jump-start," she says.

"What do you mean?"

"I sense there's a strong spirit energy here. It's a young woman. And she needs you, doesn't she, Kendall?"

I nod as I simultaneously gulp down hard.

"Sit back," Heidi instructs. "Let me give you some energy."

Hailey waits patiently, not even acknowledging Heidi's presence.

My eyes shut as I try to center my breathing and just . . . relax. Soon, I'm aware of Heidi's energy pressing into me, giving me a jolt of oomph to help me see clearly into the mind of Hailey. It's hard to put it into words exactly. It's like there's a Blooming Onion of voltage spreading across my palms, shooting massive kilowatts out in all directions.

"Holy crap! That's amazing," I shout, even though the words aren't even close to explaining what I feel. It's like Heidi attached jumper cables to me and gave my psychic battery a wicked-mondo charge. When I turn to thank her, she's not there anymore. She's quietly slipped away. That's okay. I need to attend to Hailey's needs.

I can do this now.

Visions of the young girl dance in my head, like the chorus of a Broadway musical. Flashes. Images. Memories that are hers; ones she's sharing with me. I *am* Spock. My mind-meld is complete as I watch Hailey's young life zip through my head like I lived it myself.

The watercolor of imagery appears to me. The olive green house she grew up in on Dudley Road. Her room was the one in the front with the large picture window. Her stuffed dog named Duchess was lost on a family vacation in Alexandria, Virginia, even though her father called the Howard Johnson's to see if they'd found it. A tricycle with big orange wheels that she loved so much she parked it next to her bed every night ...

The mist in my mind shifts, and Hailey's a bit older. Close to the age she appears now. Fifteen. Just a couple of years younger than I am. School's a challenge; it often is when you're an undiagnosed dyslexic. But she's having a good time with her friends. With her Jack Russell terriers, Meadow and Jacky. She's popular in her group. They hang out. Play Wii. Watch movies from downloaded torrents. Popcorn from the micro-wave and rivers of soda.

The amusement alters, though . . .

A new boy in town. Leather and a Mustang. He emanates coolness. And trouble. He's readily accepted into the clique and now her friends want to explore other options.

I gag slightly. The acrid taste of barley and hops floods the back of my mouth. Bleck! I've never been a fan of beer. That unforgettable taste is prominent in my mouth, which means it's something Hailey imbibed.

"Why?"

"We all did it," she says to me.

It's more than a rite of passage, though. I'm certainly not sitting on any kind of judgment throne. Kids do things all the time that they're not supposed to. Doesn't make it right. And in this case, it may have caused a terrible ending for Hailey.

I rush to finish this narrative. It's like reading a bestseller and not being able to turn the pages fast enough. I see Hailey. She's dressed as she is now, but her hair and makeup aren't in disarray. There's no tear in her jeans . . . yet. My head swims in the haziness that is the beer buzz she's experiencing. In my mind, I beg Hailey to show me what happened.

She's in a tree-filled area. Great. That could be anywhere.

"Show me, Hailey. Show me."

She's running now, as fast as she can, but it's not fast enough.

Is something chasing her? Does something want to hurt her? Or are they trying to stop her from harming herself? It's not clear and all I want to do is wipe away the confusion.

Then it sounds out in my ears. A scream so painfully high

that I can't believe it's wrenched out of Hailey. Her fear envelops me from head to toe. Yet I can't move. I can't see through the cobwebbed information Hailey's trying to share. Why am I not able to zero in on this and see what she's experiencing? I flail my arms around, like that's going to help. Her shriek amplifies. Which direction did it come from? All the trees look alike on my left, my right, in front of me. I know something horrible is going on with Hailey, but I can't make it out. There's only haze and confusion. I'm agonizingly aware of one thing: nothing in me can do anything to stop what's apparently happening to Hailey behind the closed curtains of my vision.

Violent coughs rip through me, and I want to throw up. Bile fills my throat and I retch dry heaves. I sputter and gag, grab at my throat like my fingers can pry open the skin and let fresh air in. Is this coming from Hailey? Did this happen to her? Or is some not-so-friendly entity thrusting yet another roadblock in my way to prevent me from helping this young girl? Just as I'm thinking that I'll pass out if someone doesn't Heimlich maneuver me, firm arms grab me and I hear my name called over and over.

"Kendall! Kendall! Damnit, talk to me!"

I force my vision to the present, pushing the mustiness of confusion away. I'm being shaken violently. Patrick stands over me, leather-clad hands clutching my upper arms. I focus on his deep, dark eyes, and the battery charge that Heidi gave me is nothing compared to this spark of radioactivity that zips between us.

After a mere second, Patrick releases me with such fierceness that I think he's pissed off. He's not, though. His gloved hand shoots to cover his mouth and then rubs at the stubble around his chin.

Hailey's gone, but not forgotten. The vision has cleared. My hacking cough has ended.

Patrick paces in front of me; he's acting as if he wants to speak, but no words leave his mouth. Shock and awe covers his face, and I read his expression like it's a text message. Then it hits me like a tsunami. "Did you see it too?"

"See what?" he asks without making eye contact.

I stand on wobbly legs, gripping the bench for support. "That . . . that vision I just had."

His annoyance returns. "What the hell were you doing out here, Kendall? What were you trying to prove?"

I place my hands on my hips defiantly. "I was connecting with the spirit I've been seeing since I got to Rose Briar."

"Yeah, well, you didn't have to go into such a deep channel."

"I wasn't channeling," I explain. "We were sort of doing a mind-meld. She was trying to show me what happened to her."

Patrick lowers his gaze to mine again but is quick to shift away and peer out at the mountains. "Her name is Hailey."

"Yes, it is," I manage to get out in a hoarse breath.

"I've seen her too."

I move my hair away from my face as my chest rises and falls

in rapid motions. "Why are we both seeing her? That vision . . .
it was . . . intense. Confusing and ambiguous, but intense.
There's something she wants me to know. I just can't grasp it."

"I can't grasp it either," he says.

"What do we do? This spirit is desperate for help."

Patrick slips his sunglasses back into place, hiding his eyes.
"And she seems to think you and I are the ones destined to
help her."

If that's the case, Lord, give me strength.

Chapter Fourteen

"Hey, you okay, Kendall?"

I roll over and squint up at my roommate. "Yeah, Jess. I was just wiped." The clock reads 6:00 and I know I need to wake up and get ready for dinner. Connecting with spirits like I did with Hailey always wears the hell out of me. It's like I ran a marathon, or two. There was no way I could go back to the conference room after something like that.

Fortunately, I had two hours of dreamless sleep.

"Did I miss anything interesting?" I ask through a yawn.

Jess reaches for her hairbrush and drags it through her blond hair. "Micah is clairvoyant, the Pucketts are all seeing, hearing, and sensing things, and Carl has been awfully good at picking lottery numbers lately."

I giggle. "I need to get some tips from him for the old college fund."

"Seriously," she says with a small snort. "The best of all though . . . you'll love it. Get this: turns out Greg Swanner has been seeing these creatures in the woods around his house."

Sitting up, I say, "Oh, yeah? Like what?"

Waving the brush around in the air, Jess says, "He was telling us this legend his grandfather told him about a witch in the area that turns into a large cat with yellow eyes that only preys on males. Apparently, Greg was out hunting with some friends and he saw this ... thing. Then he saw it one night after a football game. And he said it followed him home after a night of mud riding."

"Mud riding?" I ask.

She shrugs. "Surfing on muddy roads in your car. That's not the point, Kendall."

"Oh, sorry," I say, furrowing my brow. And I thought the nightlife in Radisson was a bit dull, what with some of the older local kids playing drunk hide-and-seek in the aisles of Mega-Mart.

Jess says, "So, Greg's the only person seeing this thing and all his pals think he's a nut ball. He's lost a lot of friends because of it. And he's like a popular guy, you know, with the football thing, and being a baseball player. He's afraid the coach is going to get word of it and kick him off the team and he won't get the scholarship he wants to the University of Alabama."

"That totally sucks," I say, feeling Greg's pain. "It's stupid what you get ostracized for."

"No kidding," she says softly.

I swing my legs off the bed and shove my feet into my flip-flops. "What did Oliver have to say?"

"Oh, he and Mary were talking about cryptozoology and

how there are so many creatures on this planet that haven't been classified. You know, like Sasquatch or Chupacabra or the Loch Ness monster?"

"Chupa-who-a?"

"Chupacabra. It translates to 'goat sucker.' It's this weird creature that's, like, part dog and part coyote and part wild boar, and it's got a spiny back and long tail."

"That sounds disgusting."

"Well, it's one of those things that people hunt and try to find."

I grin at my roomie. "You really listened in class today, didn't you."

She tosses her head and laughs. "Yeah, I did. Anyway, you totally missed it. Oliver brought out some slides of all these animals/creatures that are thought to be walking among us. Wisdom Walker has even heard of this yellow-eyed large cat that Greg is seeing. Hold on." She snags her notebook and flips the pages. "Here it is. It's called the wampus cat and it's supposed to be all over the South."

"That's the most asinine—" I stop myself, considering how many spirits I've connected with. Who's to say this wampus cat thingy doesn't really exist?

"You were saying?" Jess asks.

"Nothing. Go ahead."

"Wisdom Walker told us the story of the wampus cat. This Indian woman followed the men into the woods when they went out on the hunt. She hid under the skin of a mountain lion and listened to all the stories they told around the fire. When the men discovered her, the medicine man bound her to the cat's skin, and that's how she walks today."

"But none of Greg's other friends saw it?"

She shakes her head. "Nope. Just him. Poor guy."

"I know how he feels."

Jess reaches over and pats my knee. "You do, don't you."

"That's why we're here. We all have our burdens to bear."

"Or maybe they truly are talents, you know?" Jess tips her head to the side. "I think I understand what Oliver is talking about with this whole lifting-of-a-veil thing and our society being more open to all that's around us. It's an awfully big world. Wouldn't it be sad if we weren't sharing it with someone?"

Nodding in agreement, I say, "You have an excellent point there, my friend."

She stands and examines her teeth in the mirror, making funny faces at herself. "The cool thing is, Greg's not afraid of seeing it anymore and he doesn't care what people think. Even though he wants to go to college on scholarship, he wants to study this more. Oliver and Wisdom Walker told him he should look into classes on folklore and biology and zoology and other history. There's this paleontologist guy at the Florida Keys Community College that teaches about cryptozoology, so if Greg—or any of us—is interested in an intro, Oliver said he'd totally do it."

Stunned, I rock back and forth for a moment. "Shit. I missed everything."

"Not really," Jess notes. "Not everyone in the session fully admitted their . . . enlightenment."

My eyebrows lift in curiosity. "Oh, yeah?"

"Mr. Sunglasses and Gloves still won't fess up to anything."

"Patrick?"

"Yeah, your boyfriend," she teases. "He just sat there most of the time twirling a pen in his fingers." She stops and remembers. "Come to think of it, he bolted out of the room like Satan was on his heels at some point and didn't come back."

That would have been when he and I connected psychically or whatever it is we're doing.

Jess dives across the bed and lands next to me. "You two hooked up, didn't you!"

"No! I swear we didn't!"

Jess frowns and inspects my aura. "Damn, no pink. I was hoping for a juicy story."

"Sorry to disappoint you. No hooking up here." I stuff down the embarrassment over wanting to add the word *yet*. "I just needed some time to myself."

"Perfectly understandable, kiddo. As Oliver said from the get-go, we're all here to take from this retreat what we need. And what I need is food." She flips over in a near gymnastic move and both of her feet hit the floor. "Let's go eat! Chris is making pork tamales."

My traitorous stomach responds for me and I laugh. I swear, with the gourmet meals Chris is feeding us three times a day, I'm going to be the size of a house. Oh, well. "Bring on the food!"

After dinner, the inevitable pairing-up begins again. I guess that's just what happens when boys and girls fraternize. It's as old as Adam and Eve. Course, look where it got them.

Speedy is sleeping on the sixth step down from the inn, and the cats are out on their evening prowl. Oliver is involved in some closed-door meetings with the counselors, and the La'Costons are camped in front of their plasma television watching one of those singing-and-dancing reality contests, which I'll never understand the appeal of.

I spot Willow and TF disappearing around the back of the inn, while Micah and Jess, Greg and Harper, and Erin and Ricky all get into the hot tub, which is already bubbling and steaming at full force. I could certainly go for the relaxation of the Jacuzzi, but I don't want to be a fifth wheel.

Maddie pads by in her swimsuit, a towel draped over her arm. She stops, though, and looks like she doesn't want to interrupt the couples either. "We're thinking the same thing, aren't we?" she asks.

"Probably so," I say with a smile.

"I really love my boyfriend at home," she confesses. "He's so cute and I'd never do anything to make him not trust me."

I think for one fleeting millisecond about Jason and how I

haven't heard squat from him. I know he lives all the way up in Alaska, but last I checked, it was still one of the fifty states and people up there do have phones and Internet service. I mean, his sister found the time to text me and send me e-mails (okay, they were mostly forwarded jokes that I've seen a hundred times already, but still), and yet he can't seem to remember my phone number. Well, the hell with him!

Maddie smiles and touches my arm. "I'm sure he's thinking of you." When my eyes widen at her, she apologizes. "Sorry, it's that whole clairvoyant thing."

"No worries. Par for the course with this group." I pause for a moment and then finally admit what I've been unwilling to say out loud. Sure, I know Jason had to move to Alaska with his dad, but the breakup was inevitable. We were too different. On diverging paths. "It's okay," I tell Maddie. "I'm over him."

"Do we ever really get over that first love?" she asks seriously.

I lick my lips briefly, and without missing a beat, I say, "I certainly hope so."

My ears pick up the strains of a guitar. Maddie winks at me and giggles. "Now there's someone who's broken a lot of hearts, I bet."

"Oh, I'm sure."

With a nudge of her elbow, she says, "Maybe you should go see what you can do about mending his."

I roll my eyes and trot up the stairs toward the music—careful to step over the snoring papillon pup.

A crackling orangy-white blaze is going in the fire pit and Patrick sits with his back to me as he strums out R.E.M.'s "The One I Love."

"Anyone I know?" I ask coyly, making my presence known. "Will wonders never cease! I actually get a genuine laugh from Patrick Lynn." I flop down on the cushioned chaise next to him in victory. "Damn, I'm good."

"What*ever*, Moorehead," he says as he continues to pluck out the song. "There's no one I love other than my family. I'm too screwed up to involve myself in anyone else's life."

"Ahhh . . . he speaks out on how his abilities are affecting his world. Just what *are* his abilities, one has to wonder." I have no clue why I'm speaking like some voice-over dude, but humor seems to be the elixir that's working on this complicated guy right now.

Patrick adjusts the guitar on his thigh and stretches out his jeaned leg. He's not wearing the glasses, gloves, or knit hat. I would say his guard is seriously down right now. Not that I'm going to take advantage of it—okay, maybe just a little bit.

In the darkness, the firelight dances and casts shadows from his eyelashes onto his cheeks. His shaggy black hair blows in the slight breeze as his chocolate eyes sharpen on a distant object. I watch hypnotized as his fingers pluck the strings, sending out the song Cel, Becca, Taylor, and I have tried to master on Guitar Hero. I've got the drum part down, and Taylor is a real natural on the vocals, but Cel and Becca could totally compete against the best at playing the R.E.M. hit song. As

Patrick continues, I hum along, trying not to distract him. Instead of telling me to shush or go away, he sings softly with me, harmonizing here and there, our voices blending together in a swirling, melodious way that gives me chill bumps even though I'm sitting in front of a crackling fire.

At the end of the song, he lets his fingers dangle from the strings for a few moments. His thoughts are hidden from me; however, it seems like he's happy right now. I know I'm feeling at peace for the first time in a couple of days.

I so much want to know everything about this boy. What makes him tick? Why is he here? How can I help him? How can we help each other? How can we help Hailey?

Bravely, I ask, "Can I read you, Patrick?"

"I don't know," he says with a sexy little smirk. "Can you?"

I cross my eyes and stick out my tongue. "Thank you, Mom. *May* I read you?"

"I'd rather you not."

I lift up and lean on the end of the chaise, close to Patrick. I gather the intestinal fortitude to say what needs to be said. "We have this . . . mental tie, Patrick. You can't deny it."

"I don't," he says and then strums out a random chord. "Nor can I explain it."

"Then why can't I read you?"

He lets out a sigh and sets the guitar down to his right. His long, lean fingers slide into his thick hair, moving the strands back momentarily. I notice a few more grays at the temple, underneath the other hair. They shine in the firelight.

I toss my hands in the air. "Look, I won't beg for your story. You've heard mine. You've heard pretty much everyone else's here, yet you're shut tighter than a clam."

I have my reasons.

"I'm sure you do," I say, acknowledging what he sent to me telepathically. "I'm here to listen." Without thinking, I reach out and place my hand on the sleeve of his shirt. He doesn't flinch or move away. Instead, he adjusts back into his chair and stares into the flames. I do the same, wondering if some ethereal message will be spelled out by the conflagration and sparks.

After a few minutes, I break the silence. "We shared a moment this afternoon with the whole Hailey incident. She's reached out to both of us. How do you explain that?"

He shakes his head, tossing his hair. "I can't explain shit these days."

"That's why you're here."

Patrick snaps around to face me. "I'm here because my dad thinks I'm a freak. He called an old friend and got me into this . . . this seminar because he can't do anything for me."

"You're not a freak!" Because if you are or anyone else here is, then I am too.

You're not a freak, Kendall.

Neither are you, Patrick.

His eyes lock on mine and I sense that I won't be able to take a breath when I make the attempt. I'm paralyzed by the emotions surrounding him: fear, doubt, loneliness, confusion. I recognize them because they've been with me since I woke up in the hospital following my Sherry Biddison spill. But helping Hailey is going to get me over that hurdle. Maybe it'll cure Patrick too.

Can it? Can anything?

I want to take his hand and connect with him. I need to feel the heat of our fingers together. To solidify this union we've got going.

His beautiful brown eyes—unshielded by sunglasses finally —shift over my face, studying my nose, my eyelashes, my lips. I watch as his own lips move to form words. "I wish I could take your hand, Kendall." He turns away. "I can't, though."

I clear my throat to dislodge the emotional lump stuck right in my windpipe. "I want to know what happened, Patrick."

He shudders; no other response.

"I want to know," I reiterate forcefully and then add in my mind, *I promise not to judge or think badly of you, no matter what.*

With that, he spins back around. "That's just it, Kendall. I don't *know* what happened. I was me one moment and then the next . . . I wasn't."

I cross my legs underneath me and get comfortable. "All right. Start at the top."

Chapter Fifteen

Patrick lets out a pent-up breath and then begins his tale.

"Dad and I like to travel. He's outdoorsy and we always camp and hike and swim and stuff," he starts out. "When I was fifteen, I got my open-water SCUBA certification. It was awesome because Dad went with me on my checkout dives. We've been avid divers together for the last two years."

"That's awesome that you have something in common like that." I can't imagine being that close to either of my parents. I wonder if Emily and I would have had a special bond if she'd lived to raise me.

Patrick picks up on my lamenting about what would never happen. I urge him on with a nod.

"So, the first of the year, Dad got this deal on a trip to Barbados, so we went. It was amazing there. We did so much together."

"How fun! I bet it's gorgeous there."

"It is. The water color . . . well, I've never seen anything like it. We did the zip lines through the tree canopies of this sunken cave, and we went on a Segway tour on the northern part of the island overlooking the Atlantic."

"My best friend, Celia, has a Segway. Those things are *the* coolest," I say, wanting to connect with him even more.

"Right," he says with a smile. He really should do that more often since it makes these tiny little crinkles around his eyes that just light up my heart. "We were having a time, let me tell you. We didn't get to dive every day like we wanted to, but we had some righteous ones."

The thought of breathing underwater fascinates and frightens me at the same time. "What all did you see?"

His eyes shift into the memory. "Sea turtles, puffer fish, chum, sergeant majors; it was . . . wow."

"I bet."

A darkness overtakes his eyes. "On the third dive, I was feeling all cocky. It was a wreck dive. Nothing too complicated. It was this ship called the *Pamir* that had been deliberately sunk to make a coral reef. The sea life there was frickin' unreal."

"That would totally creep me out," I say. "Swimming around a sunken ship? Yuck!"

"It's no big deal," he assures me. "It's not like anyone died on it. They clean it up, take all the oils and toxins out of it, and it provides a home and food for the fish, coral, and plants."

I scrunch up my nose. "I suppose. So, go ahead."

"Yeah, well . . . it was a penetration dive, but I'm not certified for that."

I shift in my seat. "I don't know what that means."

Patrick licks his lips. "I'm only certified for open-water dives, which means I'm not supposed to be going in caves or ships or places like that without further training."

"Okay, that makes sense."

"It would have if I'd obeyed the rules." He scratches his head. "Like I said, I got cocky. So, when the rest of the group swam off to this small submarine that's sunk nearby, I scooted back to penetrate the wreck. It looked like a really easy one and I wanted to see what it was like."

I scowl at him. "Aren't you, like, supposed to always stay with your dive buddy? I remember seeing some program on the Travel Channel about that. Didn't your dad notice you were gone?"

Patrick hangs his head. "Yeah. It was a dick move. I thought I could penetrate and be back in a flash without anyone noticing I was gone." A long pause follows, and I know this is the part in the story where something goes wrong. "I was stupid. I went into the wreck, swam around—no big deal, right? Only problem was, my octopus regulator—the extra breathing hose you have in case your buddy or someone else runs out of air—got snagged in the lead rope that led back to the buoy on the surface. I sort of panicked and started taking in *a lot* of air. Then I pulled my dive knife from my ankle and tried to cut myself loose."

My hands move up to cover my mouth. I'm seeing everything that Patrick was going through; he's sending me images while he shares his story. I see him in his short wetsuit, his hair flowing above him in the water. His eyes are wide and panic has overtaken him.

"I must have been stuck like that a good six minutes. I totally forgot everything I'd learned in the classroom, in the textbook, and in the pool. It was the survival instinct, you know? I didn't give a damn about the bends or following my small air bubbles to the surface, I just wanted out."

"What happened?" I ask from behind my hands.

"I slashed at the lead rope to get loose, but I sliced my air hose instead."

"Oh, shit! But you had that octagon backup thingy, right?"

He chuckles. "The octopus regulator. It was stuck and I couldn't get to it. I was SOL."

"Another diving term?"

"No, Kendall, it means 'shit outta luck.'" At least he can laugh about it now. The empath in me is on the verge of tears. Even though he's sitting here with me, I'm almost afraid to hear the end of this.

"So there I am at sixty feet below with no air, no buddy, and I've got to make an emergency ascent, ASAP. In SCUBA, you're not supposed to come out of the water too fast or else you'll get the bends. I figured either I get bent or I get dead, so I kicked as hard as I could, trying to follow the lead rope back up. I grasped it so hard that I got the crap stung out of me by the sea anemone living on it."

My arm stings and itches at the same time, experiencing what he did at that moment.

"I made it to the surface and tried to inflate my buoyancy compensator—that's the jacket you wear that's attached to the tank and you can add air to it to help you float—but I'd done one heck of a job with the knife underwater, cutting not only my regulator hose but the one from the tank to the BC."

"So?"

"So, I'm at the surface where a storm had come up while we were under and I'm getting battered by the waves. I'm taking water into me in huge-ass gulps. Every time I try to get a breath, I get smacked again by a wave. I'm kicking and paddling and trying to stay on the surface. I'm looking ahead at the boat and trying to swim to it. The captain's, like, on the back under the awning to keep the rain off him and he's not paying attention to people coming out of the water. I swim so hard and . . . that's when it happens."

"What, Patrick?"

"I got tossed hard into the side of the boat and I bashed my head. Totally blacked out right there. The next thing I remember was waking up inside a hyperbaric chamber with an oxygen mask on and a massive bandage on my head."

"Holy crap! Who got you out of the water?" I ask with a bit of manicness in my voice.

"Dad and the dive master, Edwin." He closes his eyes at the retelling. "They'd been looking for me underwater and Dad was only seconds away from me when my full panic set in and I hightailed it to the surface." Patrick pounds his fists onto his knees. "It was so stupid of me to do that. I'm a trained diver.

I've got like eighteen dives under my belt. I don't know what I was thinking."

I see it clearly now. Edwin, the dive master, and Patrick's dad found him on the surface and he wasn't breathing. With the help of the boat captain, they got him up the ladder and out of his tank and jacket. Edwin performed CPR on Patrick while his father prayed over his body.

Patrick's eyes focus hard into the fire. "They tell me I was clinically dead for four and a half minutes."

I can certainly identify with that.

"I spent two days in the chamber and another three in the hospital. Ever since I woke up, I've had visions that are so painful I have to block them out. I hear voices. Not just people around me, but everyone and everything, everywhere. It's like listening to hundreds of not-quite-tuned-in radio stations. Constant chatter that pounds at my head like a woodpecker. And the worst, Kendall," he says, and then he stops for a moment.

I urge him on with a nod of my head.

"Everything I touch . . . I know everything about it. Like this bench," he says. "I can tell you the name of every person who ever sat here and where they're from and what they had for dinner that night. I know what forest the wood came from and who made it into something you can sit on. It's maddening. I can't control it and it's ruining my life."

Swallowing, I say, "That's why you wear the hat, glasses, and gloves? To block things out?"

"Yeah," he says softly. "The headphones help too. If I'm listening to music, I can pretty much keep everything else out. It's the only time I ever really have any . . . peace."

Then it all clicks. "That's why you won't get into the hot tub. Have you been back in the water since then?"

"Not really. I mean, I'm not gross. I take showers," he says with a snicker. "I can't be immersed, though. Too much rushes back. My own cowboy behavior. The betrayal to my dad and dive buddy. The damage I did to my body, that I'm now . . . cursed with seeing, hearing, and feeling every frickin' thing in the universe. I don't think I'll ever go back in the water again."

The sadness in his tone breaks my heart. I so much want to hug him right now, but I know touch is the last thing he needs.

And I thought my awakening was hard.

They're all hard. And the ones who are chosen to go through this are picked for a reason; we just have to figure out what that reason is.

"Oliver can help you."

"I know," he whispers.

"Let him."

"I'm trying."

"Let me."

He snorts. "You have your own hurdles, Kendall."

"As do you, Patrick."

I sense that he needs to be alone now, so I rise up, brush at nothing on my jeans, and stand next to him. It took a lot for him to tell me this. I'm going to say a prayer for him tonight.

For all of us, in fact. Even for that poor wampus-cat person. We could all use the good mojo. I send a thought to him that he swiftly picks up.

Thanks for sharing with me. Your secret's safe with me.

I trust you, Kendall. We're alike.

Yeah, we are.

Before I can overanalyze this or stop myself, I brush my hand delicately through the top of his hair, careful not to make too much contact. A quake runs through him and zaps me as well.

I like that, I admit.

I like you, he responds. *And* that *scares the hell out of me too.*

I take to the path and don't look back. Because if I do, I'll share too many of my thoughts and feelings with him. The ones I've tamped down as far as I can so he can't read them.

Boy, am I in trouble.

CHAPTER SIXTEEN

THURSDAY MORNING, I sit by myself in the dining area scarfing down a plate of Belgian waffles with whipped cream and fresh strawberries. I'm alone because I slept late. Jess tried to wake me up, but I slept through her pleas, as well as my BlackBerry alarm. There was not much snoozing last night; there was a lot of tossing and turning thanks to a traffic jam of spirits circling the room and my mind. Coffee just ain't gonna do it today. I totally should take a handful of B_{12} or something for energy as my ass is dragging.

Chris clears the dishes and tells me that Oliver is waiting for everyone outside. I wipe my mouth and shuffle through the inn to join the others gathered in the front. As we were instructed to do last night, we're all dressed in loose T-shirts and shorts. Mary specifically told us not to wear jewelry or watches, so I removed my diamond studs from my ears. I haven't taken them out in a couple of years, so it's, like, totally weird to be this . . . stripped. Erin Puckett is circling one wrist with the other hand and I know she's worrying about the charm bracelet she always wears. Willow's nose ring is gone, and Jess is no longer sporting her dolphin anklet. I guess we're ready.

"Any clue what's going on?" I ask my fellow retreaters.

"Not a single one," Micah says.

The crunch of tires on gravel grabs our attention. Jessica points and lets out a whoop. "Check out that suh-weet ride!"

Rolling to a stop is a spit-shined and waxed black luxury limo van.

A *swoooooosh* of the door and Oliver Bates steps out with his sunglasses in place. "Good morning, group! If everyone would please grab a towel from the rack here and come aboard, we have a small field trip that will take most of the day."

Hmm ... we weren't told to wear bathing suits, so this obviously isn't a beach excursion.

Jess and Maddie share a shrug with Erin, Harper, Willow, and me, but we obediently snap up an emerald green RBI monogrammed towel and load into the waiting ride, fanning out in a random pattern on the plush seats. The boys aren't far behind and don't seem as intrigued with our luxurious transportation as we girls are. Greg's munching on an apple that he obviously grabbed on the way out the door. Evan Christian is playing on his DSi, which is beeping away as he taps the screen. Ricky, Micah, and Carl tromp in and spread out, like boys do. Talking Feathers steps in and sits in the open seat in front of me. Finally, the elusive Patrick climbs aboard with his music blasting, and he heads straight to the back. Without saying a word or making eye contact with anyone, he lies down on the bench seat and places his forearm over his eyes. Hmm . . . he must have had a bad night too.

Glenn hands a couple of coolers to Oliver, who puts them on the front seats. "There's cold fried chicken, potato salad, fruit, granola bars, and plenty of drinks for you all," Glenn says.

Oliver nods his thanks. Then he peers down at the driver and says, "Let's get going."

It's wicked quiet as we drive through twisty-turny mountain roads. I don't know if everyone else is as tired as me or if they're merely trying to figure out what's going on. The only sound is the hum of the tires on the road and the *zug-zug-zug* of the substantial air conditioner.

"Hey, Oliver," Maddie calls, breaking the silence. "Where are we going?"

Without turning, he says, "You're psychic. Can't you figure it out?" When a devilish smirk spreads across his face, he adds, "You'll see in a little bit."

"Secretive much?" she says to her sisters.

Josiah/Talking Feathers releases a moan from deep within. I reach over the seat and put my hand on his shoulder, sensing his downright unease. It's radiating off him in waves. "You okay?"

He jumps a bit at my touch. "I'm fine. I've had a lot of spirits talking to me this morning. It seems like there's a neon sign over my cabin pointing to my abilities."

"I know the feeling," I say. I rest my chin on the seat in front of me and wonder if he's had any contact with Hailey.

"My mind was like an amusement park last night. So much Tilt-a-Whirling and swirling around, only nothing specific."

"Same here," he says. "Visions. Words. Names. Eyes. Noses. Hands. None of them add up to one person, though . . . that I know of."

Too bad Celia's not here with me. She could sketch the personages we're all seeing. I take a moment and then ask, "Do you mind if I ask about details? You know, to, like, compare notes."

Josiah cricks his neck to the left and then to the right, easing tension I can sense has built up in his muscles. "You're having spiritual visitations as well?"

"I am. One, in particular."

He stammers over his words a bit. "Look, I'm still n-new at this, so I'm not exactly sure who I'm getting. Like I said, faces and voices are jumbled together. It's like when I take my contact lenses out and everything's a blur in front of me. I can see the outlines of people and the colors they're wearing, but I can't distinguish any details or anything beyond the fog and distortion. Oliver and Heidi are working to help me focus my energies and identify who is reaching out to me."

"They're the ones who can lend a hand," I reassure him.

"I don't guess you have that problem, do you?" he asks with a near smile. One of the first I've seen from him.

"Not really. I see them, hear them, feel them, and have been severely injured because of them."

Josiah's dark eyes turn to me. "That sucks, Kendall. I heard your story the other day about the near-death experience. That would have scared me shitless. It's brave of you to keep at this."

Brave isn't exactly the adjective I'd use to describe me these days. "It's not like I have much of a choice. Just have to keep understanding this whole awakening and the best way to handle it," I say.

"Is there actually a *best* way?" he asks. "We were all chosen for a reason, I suppose."

"Yep" is all I can say and then I pat his hand.

In a gesture of friendship, Josiah turns his palm up and curls his fingers around mine for a reassuring squeeze. Two seconds later, we let go and I lean back into my seat. I feel a set of eyes on me and rotate around until I catch Patrick staring at me over the top of his sunglasses.

Is it your goal to flirt with every guy at this retreat?

Give me a break, I snap. *Besides, I don't flirt with you. You stalk me in my head.*

Whatever you say. You and Smack Talk seemed very cozy.

Jealous much?

Hardly.

And his name is Talking Feathers. Don't be a jerk!

He waits a minute. Then he says, *You know where Oliver's taking us?*

No. Do you?

Patrick pushes his sunglasses back into place and adjusts in the seat, bending one knee up and resting his hand on top of it. He peers out the window, and then I hear him in my head: *We're going to sweat.*

A few miles of rough terrain and the van stops. We're parked on a dirt road that dead-ends between some low-lying picturesque mountain ranges. The lush green of the sloping trees and swaying grass is dramatic against the aquamarine sky. The brilliant sun shimmers on the rippling surface of a good-size stream running nearby. A small, domed tentlike hut sits in the middle of the open field. It appears to be about twelve feet by twelve feet with straw covering the rounded—is that what they call thatched?—roof and a woolen blanket hanging in the cut-out opening.

"Gather around, please," Oliver instructs us once we're all off the van. "Today we have an incredible spiritual and personal ceremony for you to partake in. This is, without a doubt, my favorite activity of the whole week, and I hope you enjoy it as well. Wisdom Walker, would you?"

From around the other side of our transportation, Wisdom Walker appears in his traditional Native American garb and this gorgeous flowing headdress with feathers and beads that cascade to his waist. He could be straight off the DVD cover of *Dances with Wolves*. My breath catches in my throat as I take him in, from his moccasined feet to the thick, black braid on either side of his head.

"Oh my God," Willowmeana says, sounding almost ecstatic. "We're doing a sweat."

"All right!" Talking Feathers echoes her tone.

The rest of us just look around and then back and forth at one another in curiosity. Patrick shows no emotions, although I sense a tremor running through him.

A bead of perspiration trails down my spine, and I wish someone would tell me what "doing a sweat" means.

Oliver waves his hands in excitement. "Let's get started. We have a lot ahead of us." We all congregate around our host and listen intently. Well, at least *I* do. Anticipation runs through me like drugs through an IV line. Oliver begins to explain the task for the day and suddenly it all becomes very clear.

"Wisdom Walker and I have brought you to this sacred place for what is known in most Native American cultures as the sweat lodge ceremony."

Ahh . . . hence the sweating. Now I get it.

"For centuries, sweat baths have been used in various cultures throughout the Americas, Asia, Europe, and Africa. Native Americans use the ritual as a way of purifying themselves and remembering the traditions of their ancestors."

"This is so cool," Jessica whispers to me.

My pulse picks up as Oliver continues. "With the guidance of a medicine man, you can repair damage done to your mind, body, and spirit. A sweat lodge is a place of spiritual sanctuary, mental cleansing, and physical healing. It's a place for questions, answers, and guidance from the spirits and your totem animals."

"Oh, my friend Loreen told me about totem animals. I didn't know how you found out which one was yours," I say to the other girls.

"I did a sweat with my grandmother when I was twelve," Willow offers. "I don't remember much of it, though. Other than it being almost unbearably hot. One hint, ladies: if you need a good, cool breath, stay low to the ground."

"Right," Harper adds. "Heat rises."

Maddie pats her hair. "So much for my hairdo today."

We all snicker but then listen to Wisdom Walker as he gives more details. He points to the hut and explains.

"Sweats are held in what's called a wickiup or a tepee that's lashed together with grass or dirt, bark, or mud, like this one over here. The wickiup is held up with slender withes that are set into the ground in a circle, and they form the dome." He points at the structure like a proud architect. "It's about five feet high in the center. There's a two-by-one pit in the middle where hot rocks are placed for the steam."

"Like the sauna at the gym?" Greg asks.

"Very much so," Wisdom Walker responds.

Talking Feathers raises his hand like he's in history class. "Does it matter which way the lodge faces?"

Nodding, Wisdom Walker says, "Most sweat lodges face the east. A few feet away, you'll see we've built the sacred fire pit." I see the beginnings of a small bonfire area, but nothing has been lit. "The lodge and the pit face east, and this speaks to the rising sun that provides us with our power and life force, a dawning of wisdom to come to you. We light the fire and heat the rocks, signifying the undying radiance of the world and how each new day is a spiritual beginning."

I glance at the sacred pit he's speaking of; the stones are stacked, ready to be heated. There's also something between the door and the trench. I think it's a cow skull. Eww . . .

"We have the skull on the path to prevent anyone from stepping into the fire pit after emerging from the sweat," Oliver says, probably reading my mind.

"So, we're, like, delirious when we come out?" Ricky asks.

"You can be," Wisdom Walker explains. "It's a very moving experience."

Ricky says, "I don't know. I've heard some bad stuff about sweat lodges."

Oliver interjects, "Yes, there has been some bad press on sweating lately. However, those occurred when too many people crammed into the space and didn't come out for breaks. I assure you, I won't let that happen here."

That seems to satisfy Ricky—and me—for the moment.

Wisdom Walker continues. "And, son, we don't sweat merely once. We go in four separate times. If anyone needs to leave, he or she is free to do so."

Maddie rolls her eyes. "Seriously. I'm going to have a really bad hair day."

Erin elbows her at the same time Harper shushes her.

I'm surprised to hear Patrick ask a question. "Why do you go in four times?"

Wisdom Walker turns toward him. "Each sweat round or endurance has a significant meaning and lasts about forty-five minutes. The first endurance faces west and is for recognition of the spirit world and where we ask our Creator to let our spirit guides converse with us. The next endurance is to the north and recognizes bravery, vigor, purity, and honesty. The third is to the east, the recognition of the importance of prayer in our lives so we may gain insight in all of our activities. And the last endurance, to the south, is for growth and healing of your own spirit, using the strengths you garnered from each direction. Only then will full cleansing come to you."

Wow. That's heavy.

And this can all be achieved by merely sweating? I mean, I've sweated plenty in phys ed class and while on some pretty intense ghost hunts. I've even lost a pound or two from having the old adrenaline going. This is different, though. This will be a connection with . . . myself. A true healing and cleansing to purge the negativity, doubt, fear, and trepidation that has come into my soul. Chills cover me in my eagerness for the sweat. I giggle a little when I think of how my mom might freak out over this, believing it's some false religion and not sanctioned by the Episcopal Church. But this tradition goes back centuries and is full of positive messages, encouragement, and, above all, a connection with a higher power and faith in myself. What can be wrong with a higher consciousness of God?

"We'll explain more as we go along," Oliver says. "As Wisdom Walker said, if you're uncomfortable at all about the ceremony, you don't have to participate. The driver will take you back to the inn and no one will judge you."

A shift in the gravel draws my attention to Patrick's feet. Did he just move?

I don't think so . . .

What? he responds.

I stare him down. *You're not going anywhere. You're doing this.*

He doesn't say (or think) another word; he just stands there.

I breathe out a pent-up gust of air, feeling smug that I've kept Patrick from fleeing the terror inside himself that he will inevitably have to face. Ones we'll all have to deal with.

"Okay then," Oliver notes. "We're all in."

This is going to be a very interesting day.

Chapter Seventeen

Sparks crackle in the air, dancing around the flames in the fire pit. A warm wave reaches out to us, and the stones begin to heat.

We all take off our shoes, socks, flip-flops, or whatever covers our feet. Maddie is apparently anticipating the worst, as she's pulled her thick mane of hair into a high ponytail. I follow suit, using the elastic on my wrist to make a messy bun on top of my head.

Oliver moves around us carrying a bundle of some sort of leaves that are tightly bound and smoking. The sweet yet pungent, earthy smell swirls around each of us as Oliver passes by.

I stifle a tickle in the back of my throat that threatens to make me break out in a violent sneezing attack. "What is that?" I speak out.

"This is called smudging, and it's thought to ward away any negative energy." He takes a whiff. "It's sage. The same thing you use in a roast chicken recipe."

My mom usually uses butter, salt, pepper, and garlic with

her chicken, but I'm not going to quibble. Judging from the overpowering stench, though, I'll be passing on any sage-imbued dishes in my future dining.

Wisdom Walker follows behind Oliver, stirring the cloudy air with a large feather. "Are we all ready?"

Heads bob, and nods spread out through the group. Even a usually reserved Evan Christian seems jazzed about this, since he put his DSi away. Everyone looks as if he or she is poised on the edge of the seat.

Except Patrick.

We have to face our fears. Even you, Patrick.

I know. Eventually. When I'm ready.

They're helping us take that step now. I wait a moment and then add, *Will you sit beside me?*

With breathless anticipation, I wait for his response. *I could use a friend through this.*

"Patrick," Oliver calls out. "I need you to ditch the glasses and gloves, buddy."

I can tell by the way his body flinches at Oliver's words that he's horrified at the thought of being so . . . naked. Well, naked for him.

You can do it, Patrick. I'll be there with you.

He plucks at the fingers of his glove one by one and then crumples the leather in his fist. Slowly, he withdraws the shades, and then he hands everything over to Oliver, careful not to make any contact with the other man's skin.

Without a sound, Patrick shuffles over to my side, inching

between Jess and me. I implore her with my eyes not to say anything. Fortunately, she doesn't. We're all in an altered state, waiting for . . . whatever may come.

Using a pitchfork Wisdom Walker carefully carries the hot stones from the fire pit to the wickiup. When he's done, he strips out of his leather attire until he's wearing only a baggy pair of shorts. He motions to us and we file toward the hut. Our unintended pattern of boy-girl-boy-girl seems fine with our two leaders.

"You must crawl into the sweat lodge," Wisdom Walker instructs. "Go in a clockwise direction, and then sit cross-legged against the wall until everyone is inside and the opening sealed."

My vessels pulse under my skin in my anticipation and eagerness, coupled with, quite frankly, my being scared shitless. I'm crawling on my trembling hands and knees on the dirt and grass with Talking Feathers's butt in my face as he leads the way in. My elbows lock a bit as I move around. Yet I forge ahead. I have to do this. No turning back. I'm thirsty for a cleansing and a spiritual direction. Not that Father Mass and my parents haven't provided that along the way for me. This is more. Deeper. Darker. Sort of like how Luke Skywalker went to fight Darth Vader in the cave on Dagobah, or, in actuality, into his own dark side. Will I have a vision of slashing off some unknown enemy's head only to find my face on the decapitated portion?

Jesus, Kendall. Get a grip, I hear Patrick say in my head.

You're one to talk.

I steady my breathing and try to relax. Nothing is going to harm me. This is a good thing. We're all here together and Oliver is a responsible adult. He holds these enlightenment retreats all the time. I'm sure I would have heard if anything bad had ever happened here. I stretch out with my mind in the small space and feel the electricity in the air. There's a sensation of many souls gathering nearby to assist us. Old souls who are pleased that we're willing to take part in this ritual. I sit back against the wall of the wickiup and wait for the ceremony to begin.

Once we're all in, it's quite a tight squeeze. Oliver has remained outside, probably because he's done this a thousand times already.

Wisdom Walker shouts, "Doorkeeper, drop the flap."

And with that, the blanket covering the opening falls, and the lodge is bathed in darkness. Ahhh . . . guess that's why Oliver stayed outside.

"Now, my children," Wisdom Walker informs us, "this is a very important thing. I want you to know that if at any point you feel uncomfortable or claustrophobic or just need to leave, you are free to do so. All I ask is that you say 'all my relatives' so the others here will give you room to pass in a clockwise direction."

"What does that mean?" Ricky asks.

"It just means that you are acknowledging everyone else in

the lodge and asking to be excused. Say it with me," Wisdom Walker instructs.

"All my relatives," we say in unison.

"Very good. So, it's understood?"

A murmur of yeses, and then nothing. Total silence. I'm almost afraid to sip in a breath for fear it will be the loudest sound ever. There's nothing to dread, though. This is merely a moment-of-silence thing, like honoring the military at sports events.

The older man spreads his hands wide; he's illuminated by the red-hotness of the seven stones stacked in the middle. He begins to ladle water over the piping-hot rocks, causing steam to gush from them like a geyser. Outside, a tribal drum pounds steadily. Must be another part of Oliver's role.

"Let us pray." I bow my head and squeeze my eyes shut in the darkness. Wisdom Walker begins, his voice soothing in the shadows.

"O Great Spirit, whose voice I hear in the winds, and whose breath gives life to all of the world, hear me. I come before you, one of your many children. I am small and weak. I need your strength and wisdom. Let me walk in beauty and make my eyes ever behold the red and purple sunset. Make my hands respect the things you have made, my ears sharp to hear your voice. Make me wise, so that I may know the things you have taught my people, the lesson you have hidden in every leaf and rock. I seek strength, not to be superior to my brothers, but to be able to fight my greatest enemy—myself. Make me ever ready to come to you with clean hands and straight eyes, so when life fades as a fading sunset, my spirit will come to you without shame."

The steam surrounds me in wispy hot fingers, curling into my hair and dancing across my skin. It fills my nostrils with each breath I take, and I listen to Wisdom Walker's words.

"We are all one with the Spirit. There is no division of race, color, religion, sex. Everything is one. Each of you now has the chance to come to the Creator for healing of any pain or disease, whether it be physical, emotional, or spiritual. We will bond in a group consciousness to make sure each and every one of us has a message, a vision, to go home with."

That's a hefty promise, but how can I question the wisdom of . . . a man named Wisdom Walker?

He passes around a crooked branch that he calls the talking stick. "Please take the stick and say whatever it is that's inside of you for the group to hear."

Like we do everything else, we start clockwise, with Evan Christian taking the stick from Wisdom Walker. One by one, my friends pray for guidance, for clarity, for understanding. Some ask for forgiveness and others ask for healing. When the stick is handed from Jess to Patrick, I await his words.

I watch his Adam's apple bob up and down as he gulps hard. He wets his lips with his tongue and I urge him in my mind to be strong.

"My name is Patrick Lynn," he says a bit hoarsely. He clears his throat and then starts again. His brown eyes are like dark marbles in the nearly blackened room and I sense the effects the heat is having on him and see the beads of sweat roll down the side of his neck. "I had an . . . experience."

When he pauses and grips the stick tighter, Wisdom Walker nudges him on. "There is no judgment, Patrick. Tell us. Tell the Great Spirit what you need."

He swallows again. "I was clinically dead. It was my own stupid fault. I wasn't smart. And now I'm like . . . this." He raises his hands, palms up, the stick dropping into his lap. "Everything I touch, everything I see, everything I hear—it all talks to me. I know things I shouldn't. I don't know how to stop it or control it and it's . . . slowly driving me insane." He drops his head into his hands.

I want to reach over, but I'm unsure what that would do to him in his exposed state. No hat to block thoughts. No headphones to drown out the clamor. No gloves to obstruct my touch. So instead, I lean farther back and send up a prayer to God to please help Patrick deal with the gifts he's been given.

Patrick swipes his hands over his face. I'm not sure if he's wiping away sweat or tears. Does it really matter, though?

He passes the stick to me. Oceans of angst cover me as I struggle to find words. My name trickles out first as my thoughts cyclone into some semblance of organization.

"K-K-Kendall Moorehead." I pause as my scattered thoughts begin to settle down. "You've all heard the story of my awakening and why I'm here. The bottom line is . . . I'm scared. And I'm tired of it. I don't like being scared . . . it frightens me."

I hear a smattering of giggles in the darkness and I smile in spite of myself.

Wisdom Walker speaks. "Send it up to the Great Spirit, Kendall."

I press my lips together, feeling the blood rush out momentarily. "My spirit guide, Emily . . . my birth mother . . . has left me. She passed on, leaving me to fend for myself. Why? Why did she leave me just as we really found each other? And now . . . now . . . I have to do *this* on my own. She's not there to point me in the right direction or to act as a buffer with the belligerent spirits I encounter. She's my mother! She's supposed to protect me." Tears stream from my eyes as the steam surrounds me. Perspiration beads on my arms. My T-shirt clings to me, and I'm sure there are lovely sweat tracks showing on my sleeves and down my back. I don't care, though. This isn't a beauty contest and I'm not trying to impress. I'm trying to deal with my fear and my . . . anger. Looking into the thick steam, I say, "Emily . . . Mom . . . I can't do this without you. I need help. I'm just a kid. It's bad enough that you died and we never got to know each other. But you taught me so much and you helped me when I was ghost hunting. I need that again if I'm to continue on. Otherwise, God, please take this ability from me."

I slump, exhausted from the heat and mentally spent. I pass the stick to Josiah and completely tune out what he's saying. I want to leave. I want to spout "all my relatives" and get out of here. However, a gentle mental nudge keeps me grounded.

You're not going anywhere, Kendall.

I don't respond to Patrick's support, nor do I glance at him.

I'm here for you . . . he says.

I'm about to reach out to him when the flap of the hut is opened and sunlight pours in.

"You have completed the first endurance," Wisdom Walker says. "Exit while we replace the stones. The nearby stream will provide coolness for you."

Once out, I nab my towel and dab myself all over. Greg, Ricky, Erin, and Jess take off for the stream and jump in without hesitation. I follow and kneel on the bank, scooping the refreshing water onto my arms and legs.

A shadow falls over me and I crane my neck to see who it is, even though I know perfectly well that it's Patrick.

"You done good, Kendall," he says with a smile.

"You too," I say. "Three more to go."

CHAPTER EIGHTEEN

DURING THE OTHER SWEAT ROUNDS, I'm nearly blinded with images and visions coming to me. Not so much like the ones I have when I'm connecting with a spirit and seeing what happened to him or her. These are centered on me. The most vivid is during the third round, and in it I'm no longer in the hut. At least, that's what it feels like. I'm on top of a mountain. Clouds hang low, or perhaps I'm just that high up. Their airiness passes through me like a ghost and I'm transported to a level where I can endure anything. There is no doubt, no questioning; I have the strength to do anything. Or so it feels.

After another dunk in the stream—I've sweated off at least five pounds and those Belgian waffles from earlier—we begin the last sweat, during which we are to meditate on our totem animals.

It takes me a few minutes to get back into the groove, but the steam seems even more intense this time. My breath is hot and damp, filling my lungs and spreading through my body. Chubby droplets of perspiration crisscross down my back and my chest. My hair is wet and itchy, yet I push on. A few have left the wickiup, not able to complete the full four rounds of sweating. Maddie couldn't take it after the third round, and Greg didn't return after the second round. Poor Evan Christian left to throw up ten minutes into the third round. Everyone's okay, though, and I have to focus on myself.

Ten minutes or so passes and I'm concentrating so hard that I'm starting to get a headache behind my left eye. Suddenly, the steam in front of me clears and I'm back on the mountaintop. There are no clouds this time; nothing but cornflower blue sky for miles and miles.

A squawk catches my ear and I turn to it. A majestic bald eagle soars by, his wings lifting him past me. He circles around and then comes to stand in front of me. He turns his head and peers at me with his eye. Without speaking, the bird says he's here for me.

The eagle symbolizes a person in transition. I transcend both air and earth and am a carrier of guidance. You have many around to guide you, but you're not patient enough. I am here to help you gain patience. Only through patience will you gain understanding.

Oh . . . wow—I'm speechless and in awe. I haven't been patient through my awakening, I do realize that. I've wanted answers quickly.

The eagle flaps his wings and lifts off, hovering in front of me with his talons curled up like weapons of destruction. Steam surrounds him and I know he'll always guide and watch over me. Just like Emily was. I can utilize the eagle's energies to help guide me through situations I don't completely understand. I hear my Grandma Ethel reciting a poem she often told me when I was a little girl: "Patience is a virtue. Virtue is a grace. Both put together make a very pretty face."

And just like that, the mighty eagle before me shape-shifts, stretching out in the steam and becoming a very lovely Native American woman. Her skin is deeply tanned and her crystal green eyes radiate light. Her jet-black hair is shiny, like satin, and cascades over her shoulders. A beautiful sheer dress the color of sea foam flows around her.

"I am Anona. Emily sent me."

"My mom? Is she okay?" I ask the figure.

Anona raises her hand as if to calm me down. "She is at peace, but she heard your petition. I have been chosen as your spirit guide. I will help you with the patience you so need, Kendall."

Tears cloud my vision as I stretch my hand out to meet Anona's. Her energy and warmth encompasses me through the steam, sending vaporous fingers of security and confidence to embrace me. Perhaps I'm completely hallucinating in my heat-induced state and from all the smoking sage. But no. This is real. Anona is real. And she was sent here by Emily to watch over me.

"Will you be with me when I get home?" I ask.

Anona smiles wide. "I'm here as long as you need me, Kendall."

Relief crashes around me, a liberation of sorts. I'm no longer alone. I can face the spirits and help them in whatever way necessary. I won't be afraid. I will be patient in learning and using my abilities.

Anona blows me a kiss, and then the steam consumes her. Tension I didn't even realize I was holding in my body finally floods out through my limbs with a gentle tingle and flutter. I believe I've found peace. Whoa. Who knew that a little sweat could do this? I am armed with love from all realms—my family, my friends, my deceased relatives, animals, and my new spirit guide. Kendall Moorehead is going to be A-OK!

"No! Stop them! Stop them!" Patrick screams next to me.

I'm jerked out of my reverie and abruptly called to help him. He's in a trancelike state, staring into the steaming center of the rocks. He's twitching and holding his hands up as if to protect himself from what he's seeing.

"Stop what?" I implore him.

Wisdom Walker shifts over. "Don't shake him out of his daze. He needs to ride out the vision."

"Make them stop! Get them away," Patrick shouts.

I turn to Wisdom Walker. "Can't you do anything? He's in pain."

"Yes, he is," the older man tells me. His dark eyes zero in on me, dancing over my face. They shift to Patrick, and then back to me. A soft, gentle, and knowing smile spreads across his face, like he's aware of the connection Patrick and I have. "He needs you," he says quietly.

Without making contact, I lean over and say close to his ear, "I'm here, Patrick. It's Kendall. Show me what's happening." I place my hand on his bare shoulder; my fingers nearly burn into his sweaty skin. But I'm propelled into his vision like a bullet train, where his fear is palpable and I know I'm the only one who can lead him out of this dreadful confusion.

He shudders against me and I hear him gasp for air. With our minds locked, he tells me, *There are dolphins everywhere. They're . . . they're carrying me out deeper. Deeper out to sea.*

Stay with me, Patrick . . . hold on.

A lonely tear escapes from his eye, and I squash the desire to wipe it away. This is his terror of the water manifesting itself. Sadly, Wisdom Walker is correct. Patrick needs to ride this out.

I break from the vision to seek advice. "What does a dolphin signify, Wisdom Walker?"

"Many things," he informs me. As he talks, I listen intently so I can relay the information to Patrick. I grip his shoulder again and am thrust back into his vision.

Patrick, the dolphins aren't hurting you, I explain in the most calming voice I can muster up. *They're your totem animal. They're guiding you.*

He shakes his shaggy hair, drenched in sweat, and he screams in my head:

No!

Yes. Listen to me. The dolphins teach us harmony of mind, body, and spirit. They help balance our emotional and mental selves. They provide harmony within duality. Just like what you're going through.

You've got these abilities you have to live with now. The dolphins are trying to help you with that.

Patrick stops twitching. *They won't drown me?*

No, not at all, I transmit to him with confidence. *They protect you. They teach the value of touch as a means of support and healing. Your touch, Patrick. You see things with it. You can help others with that. Dolphins communicate through telepathy . . .* I trail off, then add, *Just like you and I communicate telepathically.*

I hear you, Kendall.

The dolphins want you to play . . . play in the water again, Patrick. They want you to live. I want you to live.

With that, Patrick's eyes pop open and we share a searing moment through the swirling steam. He nods his thanks to me, but I can see his eyes are still wild with confusion and he wants out of here to let all of this information soak in. He clears his throat and mutters the request to leave that Wisdom Walker taught us at the beginning.

"All my relatives," he says huskily.

I move back and let him pass.

"I think after the intense day we had this morning, you all deserve to do something fun," Oliver announces when we get back to the inn around one. "Wha'd'ya say we hit the beach?"

A collective whoop and holler sounds out. We all split off to our rooms to ocean up. I quickly decide to wear my pink bikini instead of my one-piece Speedo.

"I am so totally going to get some gnarly waves," Jess says.

She crams sunscreen into her bag and reaches for her shades. "Want me to teach you?"

"On what?" I ask. "You don't have a surfboard with you."

"That's okay," she says. "We'll get Oliver to take us to a beach where we can rent boards or, better yet, bodyboards. That might be a better start for you."

"Considering I've never stepped a toe into the Pacific Ocean, I don't care. I just want to say I've done it." I've been to the Gulf of Mexico one time, when I was little, and last summer, before we moved to Radisson, Dad took us all to Hilton Head on the Atlantic. I've never been out west before, so this is definitely going to be a memorable experience.

Jess laughs. "I'll take my phone and video-document the occasion."

We hightail it out of our room and meet up with the other girls. When we get to the front of the inn, the luxury liner has turned around and is waiting for us to reboard. The boys are in baggy shorts and flip-flops and ready to go. Except Patrick. Sadly, he's reverted to his old costume of a T-shirt, gloves, hat, and sunglasses. And here I thought we'd made progress this morning with the dolphins and their message to him.

I can't worry about him right now. This whole retreat has been angst and self-doubt, questioning and contemplating, finding myself and sweating. Now it's time for some fun. It *is* spring break, you know. Girl's got to come home with a little bit of a tan.

Two hours later, we pull up to the most amazingly sparkling beach I've ever seen—okay, as I said, I've only been to two beaches before. To our left is a long pier. People with fishing poles are scattered along the length with their bait in the jostling water. Waves slam into the legs of the pier with each strong gust of wind. On the beach, the tide rolls to the shore in a blasting manner, spraying the sea high into the air. I lick my lips and taste the salt on my skin.

Just as Jess thought, there are vendors renting surf- and bodyboards, as well as flippers, masks, and even kites. Evan Christian opts for a large butterfly-shaped one and heads off to sail it in the breeze. Jess, Willow, Micah, Greg, and I all rent boogie boards, and I can't wait to get in the water.

The Puckett triplets slather up in suntan oil and spread out on their beach blankets, drinking in the California goodness. Ricky and Carl don't waste a moment and race each other into the surf, disappearing under the foam.

Oliver sets up some beach chairs and a large umbrella and makes himself at home in the shade. Sadly, Patrick joins him and sticks his headphones on. I want to invite him to come frolic in the water with us; however, I know that's an exercise in futility. The ocean is no longer amusing to him. Instead of seeing it as a humongoid playground, he sees it as a harbinger of death and injury. His totem animals, the dolphins, made it abundantly clear that they want him back in the water. They want to see him play and live life to the fullest. Maybe, as the day goes on, Patrick will remember what it was like to dive and swim, and he'll come join us.

Don't count on it, Kendall.

I look around and see him holding his headphones in his hands and staring at the water numbly.

What about the sweat and what we learned?

It was just a dream. Nothing more.

I don't believe that and neither do you.

All I know is that it will take a cataclysmic event for me to get back in the ocean.

I sigh, knowing I can't convince Patrick otherwise. He'll make the move back into the water when he feels like it. When he's motivated and doesn't dread it so much.

I peel my shirt over my head and squiggle out of my shorts, tossing them onto the towel I've laid out next to Maddie. Without even having to turn, I know Patrick's eyes are on me, checking me out. A blush covers me from head to toe and I smile in his direction. He pulls his sunglasses down for a moment and then, uncharacteristically, he winks at me.

Okay, maybe he will loosen up and have some fun at the beach.

"Come on, Kendall!" Jess shouts over the roar of the ocean. "You ready to learn?"

"As ready as I'll ever be. Oh, wait! Let's do the video first."

Jess grabs her phone and clicks Record. "We are standing at the edge of the Pacific Ocean, home to sea life from here to

China, or something like that. Today, Kendall Moorehead, native of Chicago and resident of East Podunk, Georgia—"

"Radisson!" I interject.

"Whatever," Jess says with a laugh. "Today, Ms. Moorehead will be taking her very first dip into said Pacific Ocean. I am here to document this momentous occasion for all the world to see later on Facebook and YouTube."

I giggle as I edge forward to the sea. The sand crunches under my feet, and the warmth of the sun radiates down on me. "Here I go!"

A wave stretches toward me, inviting me into the turquoise water. I take several steps and then . . . *ahhhhhhh* . . . the ocean is so cooling and refreshing. Not bitterly cold like I was expecting, although it is going to take some getting used to.

"There we have it, folks," Jess says. "One small step for Kendall Moorehead, and one giant step for womankind."

We break down laughing and Jess stops the recording. "That was ridonkulous," I say.

"So what! Let me ditch this and we'll do some boogie boarding, baby!"

I wade out deeper, cringing a little as the crisp water swooshes around my bare middle. Remembering what I learned during the sweat, that I need to be braver when I face any challenge, I hold my breath and plunge under to get used to the temperature.

"Woooo!" I say when I surface.

"Attagirl," Willow says from behind me and then disappears into the surf. When she reappears, she says, "I can help Jess teach you to bodyboard."

"Thanks!" As my friend Taylor would say, this is going to be *très* fun.

We are totally having the time of our lives, kicking up water, splashing one another, and riding the massive—okay, to me they're massive—waves. In actuality, Jess says, they're only about four-foot waves, but the swells are coming about every eighteen seconds. That doesn't give us much time to swim out without having to duck under one of the waves as it rolls over us.

Micah and Greg are racing each other for each wave, both of them making it almost all the way to the shore by the end of their ride. I keep trying and trying to catch one, but my timing is off. I'm either too early with my jump and the wave crests by me or I'm too late and I never get on top of it.

Jess and Willow expertly ride almost every single swell into shore, like the boys. I'm getting wicked frustrated because everyone is catching waves but me and I want one worse than anyone.

"May I give you some advice, Kendall?" Jess asks.

"Sure thing. I need all the help I can get," I say, exasperated.

"You've got to get up on top of the wave, g'friend. Try going just a few seconds earlier and really push off the bottom, propel yourself forward. Once you get on top of the wave, hold on to the board, pressing it down some so you can ride it out."

"That's what I've been trying to do."

She shakes her head. "Not really. You're getting pounded out here. You don't want Oliver to have to come out there and rescue you, do you?"

I chuckle. "No worries. I'm a good swimmer."

I paddle out farther because I'm not going to give up. How hard can this be? Practice makes perfect.

A few failed attempts later, I'm ready to karate chop this boogie board.

"You almost had that one," Willow says as we wait for the next swell. "The waves are coming even closer, only about nine seconds apart."

"Is that good?" I ask.

"Yeah, it helps you with your timing."

Micah zooms past me, high above a wave. "Wooo-heeee!"

I slap my hand on the water. "Damnit! I want that!"

Willow smiles. "Then come with me. I'll get you on one."

Jess whizzes by in a blond flash as Willow and I continue out just past where the waves swell and peak. I sit perched on the bodyboard, facing the beach. The wind whips around me, blowing my wet hair into my eyes.

"Okay, get ready!" Willow adjusts on her board and comes over to me. "When I say go, start kicking and paddling your ass off."

I feel the sea move underneath me and feel the wave about to crest. Giving one amazing shove on the back of my board, Willow screams, "Go!" I push off the ocean floor and propel myself forward onto the board and onto the swell, kicking like I never have before. I realize I've done it. I'm on top and I'm riding in like I'm on a flying carpet.

"Oh my Gooooood!" I scream in glee. This is like nothing I've ever done. I'm skidding along on top of the water holding tight to the board, headed to the beach. Absolutely amazing! That's when I remember Jess saying something about pushing the board down . . . right? I put all of my weight forward on the board, pressing it into the water. Holy crap! I push it too far and I'm suddenly pulled under and flipped over. The water overcomes me and I don't know which way is up. Where am I? Where's the surface? I hold my breath and try to get oriented without panicking. My foot hits sand and I know that's the bottom. I thrust myself up, stretching until I finally explode to the surface.

Gaaaaasp!

No sooner do I refill my lungs with precious oxygen than another wave hits me and slams me to the bottom again. The rolling water churns me over and over like clothes spinning in the dryer. I'm totally running out of air again, but I float up just in time to gulp in more. Then another wave slams me. And another. I close my eyes against the stinging salt water that goes straight up my nose. Racking coughs hit me, as does another wave. I'm flailing around like a fish out of its tank, just waiting for that last bit of air to leave my body.

"Kendall!" Willow screams to me. "Swim, Kendall!"

What the hell does she think I'm trying to do? All I'm *doing* is swimming.

I hear Jess yelling at me as well, but I can't do anything about it.

"Help me!" I manage to screech before the next wave consumes me. I have no power over the churning sea that wants to make me part of its underwater world. Down, down, down I go again . . . bubbles smearing my vision. Something is tugging me backwards and sideways and not letting me surface.

Oh. My. God. I've already had one brush with death; am I having another? Is this the vision I saw days ago?

Seriously, this can't be how it ends for me.

CHAPTER NINETEEN

WATER RUSHES UP MY NOSE and I cough, losing precious air.

The next thing I know, someone is next to me. A hand joins with mine, and I'm tugged into the strong chest of the swimmer trying to rescue me. Jess? Willow? Maybe even Micah. Whoever it is, I'm mondo grateful.

Through the powerful kicking of my rescuer, we burst to the surface like a rocket ship. I take a deep breath, relishing the precious air inside me once again.

A muffled voice behind me says, "Hold on and don't fight me."

Like I have the strength to battle anyone, much less a person who's saving me.

I curl my hands around the muscular forearm towing me to the beach. Okay . . . so it's not one of the girls. Whatever. I don't care at this moment. I'm just glad God answered my prayers and sent me some help. I glance down. On the rippled biceps of my knight in shining armor is a small tattoo of a smiling ghost. It's both odd and soothing, and I grin because of it. Funny someone should have a tat like that.

When we reach the shore, I hear Oliver's voice. "Is she okay?"

"She'll be fine."

I sit in the shallow water and try to stop panting. I glance at the arm wrapped around my chest . . . a gloved hand holds me tightly.

Patrick.

"Ho. Ly. Shit."

He just looks at me, trying to catch his own breath.

Whoa. He overcame his fear and swam out to get me.

Patrick saved me.

Yes, I did. On both counts.

But . . . but . . . you said . . .

Your almost drowning was a cataclysmic event, Kendall.

I twist in his arms until we're eye to eye. Heart to heart. Soul to soul. Then, without caring what he—or anyone else— will think about me, I throw myself around him and hug him with the remaining ounces of strength that I have. He pulls me in tightly and squeezes back.

Thanks *sounds incredibly lame . . . but thanks.*

De nada.

He sets me back away from him and smiles. It is both heart- breaking and liberating. His eyes soften and I read pages of concern from him. He cares about me and risked everything by jumping into the water. I'm lost in the complexities of his face, and thoughts of Jason Tillson up in Alaska fade into oblivion.

I realize that although Patrick saved me from the water, I'm totally a goner over him.

"I really do think we should call the doctor to come check on you, dear," Chris says when we're back at the inn. She ladles another gigamonic mound of her homemade beef stew into my bowl. Apparently the rule is starve a fever, feed the nearly drowned.

Blowing on the molten stew, I say, "I'm fine. Seriously. No doctor, please."

Maddie tilts her head to one side. "Doctors make house calls out here?"

Chris nods. "They do when they're your brother-in-law."

I smile sweetly at the innkeeper. "That's awfully nice of you, Miss Chris, but I'm okay. I just won't need sodium in my food for a while after all the salt water I consumed today."

Everyone around laughs. Even Patrick.

I'm still in shock that he jumped into the water and saved me. I'm forever in his debt.

He lifts his head up from his food and fixes his gaze on me. No sentences pass between us. Not even thoughts. Nothing needs to be said. Words don't matter. Only feelings. I'm all atingle and it's not from the seawater buzz I've had all afternoon.

It's from Patrick. We share ... something. Souls that were meant to cross? I don't even want to think about what might have happened to me if he hadn't jumped into the water. I might have been fish food for all of the Pacific Ocean's marine life.

Oliver lets out a sigh of relief. "I think, considering the physical exertion of the day, we'll call it an early one. We'll reconvene in the morning, okay?"

"It's only seven thirty," Greg says in a slight whine.

I feel like a buzz kill on the retreat, but all I want to do is crawl into the cool sheets of my comfy bed and try not to think about the close call I had. If it weren't for Patrick ...

Well, I don't want to think about it. With one last look tossed at my rescuer—and a wink from him—I go over to Jess, she wraps her arm around my shoulder, and we head off to cabin 14.

Sleep doesn't last long, though.

Tap, tap, tap.

I roll over in bed to see what Jessica is up to. She's sound asleep, her leg slung over the covers and hanging off the bed.

Tap, tap, tap.

"What the—"

The clock reads 11:11, and I am so not happy to be awakened. Whatever spirit is messing with me right now needs to understand the physically and emotionally exhausting day I've had.

Kendall . . . it's me.

Patrick?

I slip on my RHS shorts and grab my blue sweatshirt, then creep over to the door. The moonlight streams into the room when I crack it open. Patrick is standing on the porch in a long-sleeved shirt that reads "I Love the Smell of Neoprene in the Morning." I have no earthly clue what that even means.

"It's a diving reference," he says in response to my thoughts. "That's not important, though. I need to talk to you."

Crossing my arms over my chest, I follow him out into the night. He's not wearing his hat or sunglasses, but the leather gloves are still on.

He spins to face me. "Look, I got a visit from Hailey a little while ago."

"My Hailey?"

"Unless you know of another teenage spirit that's hanging around here tapping on both of our minds."

"Sorry," I say. "What did she want?"

"She told me she's been missing for months. Her parents are still holding out hope, but it's false hope, since she's a ghost. We've got to help her . . . somehow."

"What can we do?" I ask.

"I don't know. We've got to do something. There's a restless spirit and a family out there that needs closure."

Striking out onto the path, I say, "We've got to tell the counselors."

"I'm right behind you."

We pad through the garden area and up the long staircase.

Once inside the main house, we're greeted by a yelping Speedy, growling and snarling at us like we're burglars.

"Calm down, puppy," I say as he wags his fluffy tail at me.

"You'll wake the whole compound," Patrick fusses at him.

Speedy nips at our legs as we make our way into the sitting room of the inn. Chris and Glenn share a bedroom here on the first floor, but I'm not exactly sure where Heidi, Mary, Peggy, and Wisdom Walker sleep.

"Down this hall," Patrick says and leads the way.

Sure enough, there are more guest rooms off the pitch-black hallway. Yet when we knock on a door, no one answers.

"Try the next one," I encourage.

No answer on that one either.

Speedy's guard-dog yapping has awakened the innkeepers. Chris comes out of her room in a flowery bathrobe. "What are you kids doing up this late?"

"We're looking for the counselors," I say.

Chris eyeballs us both and then looks at Speedy, who adds an extra growl. "Now don't go getting hinky on these children, Speedy. Back outside. Shoo!" Chris closes the bedroom door behind her and then flicks on the hall light. "Come out to the kitchen and I'll get Oliver."

I furrow my brow. "Oh, geesh—we didn't want to bother him. Can't you tell us where Peggy and Heidi are?"

"They're . . . umm . . . not here right now," Chris says. She moves to the coffeemaker and switches it on. "They don't always stay here."

"Oh," I say, dejected. Of course, if they live in the area, it would be silly for them to live here; they probably have families of their own.

"Please get Oliver then," Patrick says.

Soon, Oliver enters the kitchen, dark circles under his eyes from sleep interruption. Patrick and I relay everything we know about Hailey—how she approached us both here, the visions we've had, and how she's pleaded for help.

Oliver scratches his chin with his thumb and forefinger. "Can either of you draw me a picture of her?"

I frown. "I can't even draw stick figures, I'm afraid."

"Me either," Patrick says.

Oliver thinks hard. "I don't remember the ability to draw being in any attendee's dossier. If I had a rendering of her, I could get it out to the authorities and see what we could find out."

Aha!

"I know! My best friend, Celia, is an amazing artist. She can do it."

Oliver cocks an eyebrow at me. "There are plenty of local police forces we could go to who have artists who can—"

"She'll *want* to help, Oliver. Hailey's missing body could be anywhere. We have no idea if it's a local case or not."

"That's true," he says.

"Besides," I say with a knowing snicker, "if I don't go to Celia for help, I'd never hear the end of it."

"Okay, then," he says. "Where is she?"

"She's in Chicago with her family, but I can Skype her on the computer," I say, not even thinking of the hour and the time diff.

"Sounds perfect."

Patrick and I leave Oliver and head back to my room. Without any thought of Jess slumbering away, I snatch on the light and pull my computer up onto the bed. Patrick sits next to me and waits patiently as the laptop boots up. Jess groans and mumbles something, then turns her back to us. That girl could sleep through a tornado, I bet.

The call on Skype goes through to Celia_GhostHuntress, and after five rings, a very disheveled and sleepy Celia appears on the screen.

"Are you effing kidding me, K? It's like one a.m."

"Sorry, Cel! This is an emergency and I knew you'd want to help." I tell her over the webcam what's going on with Hailey. "So, as you can see, I need your drawing services ASAP."

The lamp next to Celia's bed comes on and soon she's in full ghost-huntress mode. "Ready when you are."

"Oh, Cel, by the way, this is Patrick Lynn. He's seen this spirit too, so we'll both be describing her to you."

Celia's eyes twinkle a bit and I can read six thousand questions scrolling in her mind like a Wall Street ticker board. "Nice to meet you, Patrick."

For the next hour, he and I take turns telling Celia about

Hailey: her features, her outfit, and her hair. Celia's tongue pokes out of her mouth as she puts the final touches on the picture and then holds it up to the screen.

"How's that?" she asks.

"Perfect!" Patrick and I say at exactly the same time.

"How do we get that to Oliver?" he asks.

"Ahhh . . . I know. Cel, hold it up to the screen again." When she does, I move my mouse to the top of the screen and click Take Snapshot. "Voilà!"

"That's pretty cool," Patrick says and then smiles. "Great job, Celia. Nice to meet you."

"You too, Patrick," she says. "Umm . . . Kendall, you owe me one hell of a phone call."

"Later, Cel. You're the best! Love ya; mean it."

Patrick and I rush back to the main inn with my laptop in tow. Oliver is sipping coffee at the kitchen table and reading a book of meditations. We plug my computer into the printer port in the sitting area where the guest computer is, and the image of Hailey prints out.

Oliver takes the page and studies it; his hands hover over Hailey's features. "I'm getting strong energy from her. While you were right to assume this case could be anywhere, I believe it *is* local and that's why Hailey reached out to the two of you. You definitely have something here." He glances at us. "I'll get this to my connections in the police department and see what we can discover. See if your Hailey here matches any missing-persons cases."

"Thanks, Oliver," I say and then move to return to my cabin.

"Since we're awake, let's stir the whole team and get them on this too," Oliver says as he stands up. "Might as well use all the psychic brainpower we've got here."

"I'll get the girls," I say excitedly.

"I'll get the guys," Patrick echoes.

He walks back with me as we get ready to wake up the whole complex. There's so much I want to say to him, but my thoughts back up like a clogged drain. At my porch, he gazes down on me with those incredible brown eyes of his. I swear he wants to kiss me.

And I want to kiss him back.

He reaches his gloved hand up to my cheek, but pulls away before making actual contact. He shoves his hand into the pocket of his jeans.

"See you in a bit, Kendall."

And with that, he disappears around the corner, leaving me breathless.

CHAPTER TWENTY

THIRTY MINUTES LATER, an unkempt and slightly sleep-discombobulated group sits in the conference room awaiting instructions.

Oliver bounds in with another steaming cup of coffee, excitement simply radiating off him. "I know I called it an early night, but something's come up and I need everyone's help, energies, and abilities. We have some work to do."

Several of my friends moan and groan in their sleep haze.

"Awww, come on, y'all," Harper says. "We're here to learn."

"Exactly," Oliver says. "This is not only a challenge of your collective abilities and enlightenment but a chance to help a family whose daughter has been missing for several months. We may be able to solve this as a group."

"I wasn't asleep," Micah says. "I was just surfing the Web."

"We're here," Peggy announces, and Mary, Heidi, and Wisdom Walker follow her into the room.

"Good, good," Oliver says. "Let's get settled, then."

I grab a Diet Coke from the refreshment table that Chris

and Glenn set up and then sit next to Patrick, awaiting Oliver's next directive.

While our host elucidates all the details Patrick and I told him, I try not to be geeked out that Patrick has looped his arm over the back of my chair. This isn't the time for my immense crush on him. It's time to join together as a group to help find Hailey. Like she asked me to do. And like Emily told me to do.

Oliver clicks on an overhead projector, and the sketched image that Celia was kind enough to make appears on the screen.

"Both Patrick and Kendall have had visitations from this spirit while here at Rose Briar Inn. Has anyone else had contact with her?"

Willow raises her hand. "I felt the presence of an owl here. He's been speaking to me. He told me of a teenage girl who was . . . lost, but it was so vague, I didn't know what to do with that, eh?"

"Okay, good, good," Oliver says with a nod. "Yes, Harper?"

Harper is slow to speak, then says, "I've been experiencing some crazy empathic feelings."

Oliver frowns. "Did you discuss it with any of the counselors?"

"I did," she says softly. "Peggy, Mary, and I talked about it. I didn't have anything concrete to go on, so we just used it as a discussion. Thing is, though, the pain I've been getting is up here." Harper moves her hands to her neck. "It's definitely a strangulation sensation. No doubt about it."

Patrick and I share a glance. Strangulation?

Talking Feathers lifts his hand high. "Kendall and I talked about seeing a spirit, but we didn't compare notes. I don't know specifics, only that it's a young girl and murder was the cause of her death."

Murder? I wasn't getting anything like that. "Why didn't Hailey tell *me* that?"

Shaking his head, Talking Feathers says, "I can't explain it."

Oliver is obviously very excited. "But wait—there's more." He moves the projector a little bit to the left so he's standing in the middle of the room in front of us. "When Patrick and Kendall came to me with this image, I took the liberty of faxing it to my contacts in several law enforcement agencies that have national databases on missing persons."

"And?" I ask, literally on the edge of my seat.

"Kendall, we got a hit." Oliver grins like a proud parent. Peggy, Mary, and Heidi all clap and exchange whispers.

"That quickly?"

"Like I said, I have ... people."

Patrick nudges me with his elbow.

Oliver continues. "The picture matches the description and photos of a missing teenager from Calistoga, California—north of San Francisco. Her name is Hailey Ann Santiago, and she's been gone for three months. Her last known whereabouts was with a group of friends who went hiking over Christmas break in wine country. All of the friends and family were interrogated, and every one of them had the same story. They dropped her off at home that day and never saw her again. Each one of them passed polygraphs, so the trail went cold and there aren't many more details to date. It's interesting that a girl who comes from northern California and who disappeared there would be showing herself in visions to us here in central California." Oliver pauses to contemplate this for a moment. "I want you all to concentrate on this picture. Use your abilities, whatever they may be, to connect with Hailey's spirit. We want to help the authorities find her body so we can bring closure to her family."

Oliver passes out copies of Celia's drawing of Hailey to us, and I stifle a gag thinking of poor Hailey lost somewhere, decomposing to the point where her family may not be able to identify her. My chest aches like I've got cinder blocks on me at what the girl must have gone through. How could something so terrible happen?

Patrick taps my chair with his foot. "We'll solve this, Kendall. We'll get Hailey home. I promise."

Peggy, Mary, and Heidi fan out around the room and we form small groups. The Puckett triplets set out to connect with Hailey through their clairvoyance, clairaudience, and empathic abilities. Willow and Talking Feathers split off, and I hear Mary instructing them on how to channel Hailey through automatic writing. Evan Christian and Carl pair up to see what they can come up with using a dowsing pendulum. Patrick and I don't move.

Heidi approaches us. "You two must have the strongest

connection with Hailey, since you've both seen and talked to her. Perhaps we can meditate together and see if she will come through to you."

"Sure thing," I say. "Whatever we need to do. I have my pendulum. We could do some dowsing too."

Patrick shakes his head. "We need to do more than that, Kendall."

It's clear. We need to lock brains like we've done so many times before and see if two heads are better than one.

Heidi motions to some bulky pillows on the floor in the corner of the room. "Down here, kids. Get comfortable."

We do as she says, facing each other. I reach my hands out to Patrick, knowing we'll get more psychic energy this way. At first, he shakes his head no.

Emphatically, I shove my hands farther toward him. "Patrick, we're connected. You can't deny that. We *have* to do this for Hailey."

He lets out a long sigh and runs his hands through his hair. Slowly, he peels off his leather gloves and sets them in his lap. Then he stretches his hands to me.

"I'll spread some Reiki energy around the two of you," Heidi says.

Neither one of us acknowledges her as we stare into each other's eyes. With a hushed sigh from each of us, Patrick and I join our hands together. An immediate buzz covers my skin, making the hairs on my arms stand at attention. An electric current zaps through me, much like lightning filling the sky. I know he feels it too. There's no denying it from the expression of wonderment on his gorgeous face.

I close my eyes and watch the images that our minds are producing. Neither of us says anything; we just sit back and watch as the mystery unfolds before us. The energy coming from our hands and minds circles us in an invisible ring of psychic power. Things I haven't been able to see on my own—and Patrick hasn't been able to decipher alone—suddenly click into place, like a key in a lock. The vision shifts and settles into lucid images that he and I can both discern.

We're walking through a gate at a national park.

Look at the giant trees, he points out. *We could be anywhere in California.*

We could be anywhere. Period.

No, we're in California.

Yes, he's right. Massive trees that reach to the heavens stand before us everywhere. I've never seen trees so big in my life. Under our feet, there's the crunch of gravel and dirt and leaves as we walk through this tree park. The trunks of these mammoth beasts are forty feet around! At the base of one on the pathway, I stop.

Patrick's hands tighten on mine.

Hailey is here. Her energy is everywhere.

I feel her too, I confirm.

And then we see her up ahead. I'm not sure if it's residual energy that's playing back like a movie for our benefit or if we've actually catapulted ourselves into the time when Hailey suffered at the hand of another. Either way, we're seeing her. We are psychic witnesses to the violence about to befall her.

Sure enough, there's someone with her, hiking up ahead and forcing her along. I see boots . . . Timberlands, I think. Brown and well-worn. The smell of beer permeates the air. We're tromping along with them through the paths and trees, deeper and deeper into the forest. We see . . . everything . . . everything Hailey sees as she's struggling behind this person.

We have to keep up with them. I begin to choke up, but Patrick tightens his grip for a moment.

Stay with me, Kendall. We need more information. Where is she going?

Is he forcing her?

I feel fear, annoyance, and confusion from her.

I need more help, Patrick.

I plead to my new spirit guide, if she's listening. *Anona . . . are you with me? Please give me a clue. Anything.* Mist forms in my mind's eye and then clears to give me two vivid images. The first is of a butterfly fluttering around, and the second is a Spanish textbook.

Patrick slumps. *A butterfly and a book? What does that even mean, Kendall?*

Shhh . . . let me figure it out. Butterfly . . . fly . . . flutter . . . wings . . . larva . . . cocoon . . . book, learn, teach, school . . .

Kendall . . . for Christ's sake!

Wait! This isn't for me, it's for you. Did you take Spanish in school?

Two semesters, sophomore year.

What is Spanish for butterfly?

Umm . . . mariposa. *Why?*

Is there anyplace near here called that? One that has these giga-monic trees?

Patrick's hands squeeze mine again. *You're brilliant! Mariposa Grove. That's where the giant sequoias are.*

And that's where? I ask, feeling stupid that I don't know.

Yosemite. Like . . . an hour from here.

The vision breaks and Patrick and I find ourselves staring at each other, nearly panting in exhaustion from our connection.

Heidi joins our space. "Anything?"

"Everything," I say with a smile.

"At least a place to start looking," Patrick notes.

"Oliver," Heidi calls out. "We have another hit."

Patrick and I just sit there, smiling at each other. No words are spoken. None are necessary. I try to pull my hands away, thinking he'll want to don his gloves again. However, he weaves his fingers tightly with mine, in a comforting, soothing, ro-mantic way.

"I don't need the gloves anymore," he says.

Everything has changed.

CHAPTER TWENTY-ONE

"YOU DIDN'T SLEEP MUCH," Jess says to me on our way to break-fast the next morning. We seem to have this conversation every day.

"Nope. Neither did you, huh?"

"Not really. I was seeing this blinding lemon yellow aura radiating off Hailey's picture," Jess explains.

I scrunch up my face. "Inanimate objects have auras?"

Jess shakes her head. "Honey, in my world *everything* has an aura. It's insane. Why do you think I'm here?" Then she adds, "Peggy said that means Hailey was struggling to maintain power or control in a relationship, and she had a fear of losing control. Did she have a boyfriend?"

"I had a vision of one, but that was sort of a conglomera-tion of Hailey's past in general. I can't assume he was in the picture when she disappeared."

In the main inn, we totally bypass the bounty of fruits, quiches, and juice laid out on the table and head straight down to the conference room. A lot of the other kids are there too, working on the case. Oliver is resting his chin on his hands, studying some papers before him.

"Anything?" I ask.

Oliver lifts his eyes up and peers at me. "The information you and Patrick came up with last night was key. Willow also got something good out of her automatic writing. She got an ex-boyfriend picking Hailey up at her house in Calistoga after her friends dropped her off. He had had a lot of beer, and there was a lot of gas in the car for a long road trip."

Jess smacks my arm. "I *told* you there was a boyfriend. Damn, I'm good." She explains her aura readings to Oliver.

"That's consistent with everything else we've gathered from you kids. I was on the phone earlier with the authorities up at Yosemite. This time of year, not all of the roads are open to visitors. However, due to my reputation, they've granted us access to the park. We've been asked to keep a low profile. The mini-coach will be here momentarily and we'll get going to the park." Oliver pats me on the arm.

"I always wanted to see the giant sequoias," I say to Jess. "Never thought it would be to solve a murder."

The ride from the inn to the south gate of Yosemite National Park takes about an hour. Time for me to prepare for what we might find. The scenery is a bit distracting, though. It's so breathtakingly beautiful up here it's not even funny. Even this time of year, there's snow on the mountain peaks in the distance, but there's also wildflowers scattered about. I've never seen trees like this ever before in my life. It's insane how tall they are. Pine trees in Radisson have *nothing* on these gigantic beasts.

We're met at the gate by a park ranger named Colin Allen. "There are two sheriff's deputies up the drive there to meet you. Plainclothes."

"I understand," Oliver says, and then climbs back in the coach.

The driver heads to the right, and the van chugs up the steep incline into Mariposa Grove, where the sequoias are.

Behind me, Patrick gazes out the window. I turn to him and ask, "Is it weird that I want to be wrong about what we saw in our vision?"

He screws up his mouth. "No, not weird at all. But aren't most of your visions pretty accurate?"

I nod. "If this one is, it means that a girl my age was murdered and left for dead. That's not exactly something I *see* on a daily basis. I usually just read tarot cards or help Celia, Taylor, and Becca point the EMF detector in the direction of the spirit I'm feeling."

"You're doing what you were destined to do, Kendall," Patrick says and offers me his bare hand. I take it and lace my fingers with his.

"I know. Hailey's a spirit in transition. I want to help her pass into the light."

"Me too." Patrick lifts our joined hands and places them on his knee. "We'll do it together."

Before I can put my other hand over his, the van jolts to a stop and the door whooshes open. Oliver stands at the front and addresses all of us.

"First off," he starts, "I want to tell you what a special group you are. I've never had a retreat take such a turn as this. Considering what I do as a career, *Ethereal Evidence*, I'm pleased that we might be able to solve the missing-persons case of Hailey Santiago and bring closure to her family up in Calistoga." He paces. "Now, this isn't going to be for all of you and I'm not forcing anyone to come along with this. You all have different talents and abilities. And many of you have helped already. Evan Christian, you knew to look at her Facebook page, which had a lot of information and links to pictures of friends and such. Josiah, you and Willow gave us details with the automatic writing, and the Puckett girls really connected with what Hailey was feeling in her last moments. I'd like you all to come, but it's up to you. This will certainly be dirty and tiring, and it may also be painful for you. I won't hide that fact."

In a no-brainer, Patrick and I move to the front of the van, followed by Willow, Jessica, Greg, Micah, and Talking Feathers. Soon, the Pucketts join us, along with Carl, Evan Christian, and Ricky. A united front.

"Very nice," Oliver says. "I'm very proud of you."

We all nod.

"Okay. Patrick and Kendall, lead the way."

Evan Christian grabs his backpack and pats it. "I printed out the pictures from her Facebook page in case you want to take them with you. There might be something in there that we can use to help us."

Oliver tousles his hair. "Good thinking."

"Ready?" Patrick asks, offering me his hand again.

I smile broadly and lace my fingers with his. "Let's go."

Oliver had told us in previous discussions that he doesn't usually get involved in a case unless the police contact him. Nothing like having a psychic call and say "Hey, I know where the dead body is" to put said psychic at the top of the who-done-it list. Fortunately, that's not the case here. Oliver's reputation from his television show, as well as his connections with national law enforcement, have made it possible for us to come in here unquestioned and try to lead the authorities to Hailey's body. These are certainly extenuating circumstances.

We hike the path through Mariposa Grove, past a fallen be-hemoth that is like a piece of a skyscraper lying on its side. On another occasion, I want to come back here to take pictures—maybe with Taylor Tillson—and appreciate my surroundings. Now, all I can think of is Hailey and what she was going through in her last moments.

"She was here," Patrick says. He touches the exposed root of the tree. "She stood here, laughing, and took several pictures. They were buzzed from the beer and kidding around."

"Do you know who was with her?" one of the sheriff's deputies asks.

"It's not clear right now, sir," he says. "It's a male, I'm feeling."

We continue. Anona comes to me and gives me what she calls a clue.

"Why would my spirit guide be showing me a single red rose?" I ask to Patrick and Oliver.

Willow snickers. "Does she watch *The Bachelor*?"

I try not to laugh in this solemn moment, but humor has always been key in my investigation with my ghost huntresses. Of course, Celia would have a comeback, like in *The Merchant of Venice* where the Bard writes, "Goodly Lord, what a wit-snapper are you!" But wait—she has something . . .

"Talking Feathers, may I borrow your park map?" He hands it to me, and I drag my finger over the black marked trails until I see one labeled *Bachelor and Three Graces*. "We have to go here," I say, pointing.

"Lead the way," Oliver says.

I'm nearly out of breath when we reach the large "male" sequoia with three smaller "female" trees next to it. I move to stand between the bachelor and his three graces and I suddenly fall to my knees. It's like that time in ninth grade when I fell down the hill next to the church and had the wind knocked out of me. I struggle to get a good breath. Patrick rushes to my side, but Oliver holds him off.

"She's getting something," Oliver says.

"It-it-it started here," I say carefully.

"What happened?"

"The argument," I say. "Hailey is arguing with a guy. They're both ... drunk."

"The guy with the brown Timberlands?" Patrick asks.

"Yeah. It's him."

Oliver closes his eyes. "I feel their energy too. Go on, Kendall."

Patrick helps me to my feet and we stand among the trees, gripping hands. I begin to see flashes of the movie that is Hailey's last day. "She's really pissed off and doesn't want to be here. He ambushed her at her house when her friends dropped her off after their hike. They drove all night to get down here. I can't see the car."

"I can," Patrick says. "Blue Mustang from the nineties. California plates, but I can't make out the letters."

Maddie interjects, "She knew him. They'd been involved. But they broke up and he sort of lost control over losing her. He brought her here hoping to win her back with the beauty of the scenery."

"Right, but Hailey just wanted to go home," Micah adds. He stops and glances at the trees. "She knew something wasn't cool. He took her cell phone from her."

Patrick points to the road. "Hailey broke away from him. That's the residual energy Oliver is feeling. It's from their fight. He grabbed at her and Hailey took off running. That way."

Without another word, we return to the path and continue.

Hailey must have been in really good shape because we keep going and going and going until we reach the fallen Wawona Tunnel Tree.

"You used to be able to drive your car through here," Ranger Allen reports.

"They were here," I say. "The argument got more heated. He took a swing at her. Hailey lunged at him and he pushed her back." My eyes cloud with the images I'm seeing of hands gripping Hailey fiercely.

Erin chimes in. "There's a class ring on the left hand of the guy. Large red stone. Like a garnet or something. This guy is losing his shit."

"I'm trying to scream," Harper says. "Hailey, I mean. I'm feeling her attempt to scream, but it's not working because his hands are over her mouth."

An owl squawks overhead and takes flight. Willow watches his pattern and then looks to all of us, knowing the owl is a sign.

Patrick takes over. "Now his hands are around Hailey's throat and she's struggling to breathe. Her eyes are begging him to stop."

I blink hard to rid my own eyes of the hot tears filming my vision. "She died here. He panicked and hid her body. The ground was hard, so he couldn't bury her deep. But she's here."

The policemen take notice. "We need something more substantial."

Oliver raises his hand. "Give them a moment, Officers."

"I have divining rods," Talking Feathers says. "Let me walk around the area some."

"I'll dowse," Carl says.

"I'll dowse too," I say.

Harper stoops to the ground and begins to feel around, obviously trying to connect with Hailey or her attacker.

With Carl and me dowsing with pendulums, Josiah on the rods, Harper using her empathy, and Patrick and Oliver going purely by instinct, we all end up in the same exact location.

"Look!" Willow exclaims, pointing up. Sure enough, the owl is on the branch of the nearest tree, watching us. "It's a sign."

"It damn sure is," Patrick says.

We exchange glances, wondering what to do next. We're in a thick covering of leaves and pinecones, about fifty feet east of the Wawona Tunnel Tree. It's far off the path, in an area where tourists would never venture; no wonder Hailey hasn't been discovered. But she is here.

You found me, Kendall, Hailey says, standing next to me.

Why didn't you just tell me? I ask. *Wouldn't that have been easier?*

She shrugs. *I didn't know where I was. I was scared and confused. But I knew you'd help. You and Patrick. You have a special bond and you used it to find me.*

Patrick's fingers tighten on my hand, and I know he sees her too.

His voice is mature and calm, not bitter or denying now. "Oliver, get the policemen, please."

No one moves. Certainly not me. While I talk to spirits all the time, I certainly don't want to see a dead body.

The deputies rush over and confer with Oliver. One of the men breaks off and asks us to leave the area. My tears fall unfettered now as I bury my head in Patrick's shoulder. He holds me closely, stroking my hair with his firm hand. A shudder passes through him, letting me know he's not untouched by what we've just been through.

"We did what we were supposed to do," he whispers.

The crunch of leaves alerts us to Oliver's return. "They've found a body. Just where we said it would be. It's extremely decayed, but it looks to be that of a young woman."

Sobbing openly, I cling to Patrick and mourn the girl I never knew and the family who lost her over a jealous boyfriend. I wish I could see him. I've seen his car, his boots, and that class ring. I wish—wait!

"Where's Evan Christian?"

I hear a rustling from behind. "Right here, Kendall."

"I need the pics you printed out."

He reaches into his backpack and draws out the thick stack. I snatch them away without thanking him. I spread them on the forest floor and get on my knees to get a better look. Erin and Harper join me. The ones of Hailey and her girlfriends and parents don't matter. I toss them aside. "Come on . . ."

There it is. The Holy Grail, so to speak.

Hailey is cuddled up with a good-looking older guy who's standing next to a blue Mustang. She looks so happy and in love. He's gorgeous and knows he's scored with a babe like Hailey. My eyes move down to the worn brown hiking boots. Only one thing remains to be seen.

"I wish I had a magnifying glass. Damnit!"

Ranger Allen steps forward. "I've got one, miss. I have it to show the kids on tours how you can use the sun to make a spark."

I'd totally hug this ranger if I weren't so desperate to get a closer look at this picture. I take the small glass and hold it close to the paper, pulling back slightly to look at his left hand. Sure enough, there's a ring with a red stone in the middle of it.

The caption of the picture reads *Me and Derrick at Stacey's Going-Away Party*.

"Oliver, this is the guy. His name is Derrick. I'm sure this is who killed her."

Our host takes the picture from me and nods. "You've done a great job, Kendall. All of you, in fact. We'll let the authorities handle it now."

Chapter Twenty-two

The mini-coach turns into the inn and we're greeted by Chris, Glenn, Speedy, and a couple of the cats. I'm so frickin' exhausted, it's not even funny. What happened in Yosemite completely drained every bit of energy out of me. Patrick had to help me walk back to the coach from the murder site, and once in my seat, I promptly slipped into a low-grade coma.

But we found Hailey. We. Found. Her.

Glenn helps me down now and pats me on the back. Chris hugs me to her. "I hear you kids accomplished quite a feat. I'm so proud of you!"

"Thanks," I say.

She proceeds to hug everyone; even Patrick accepts her warmth.

"I'll have a late lunch ready in no time."

"I'm famished," Maddie announces.

Harper nods. "Me too, although I barely did anything out there."

"Look," I say to her. "You were feeling Hailey's pain, too.

You *did* help. You confirmed what other people were sensing. Don't downplay that, g'friend."

"Where are the counselors?" Patrick asks. "I want to tell them what happened."

Oliver's face brightens. "Then let's go to the conference room and fill them in."

"Geesh, you think they would have been out here for the welcome wagon," Jess says a bit snarkily.

"Yeah," Greg agrees. "It's like they're vampires. Hey! Maybe they are!"

"Get over it, Gregory," Maddie says, ever the flirt.

Downstairs, Mary, Heidi, Peggy, and Wisdom Walker are waiting for us. "We just got word that the police identified Hailey," Peggy says. "They're calling her parents in Calistoga."

"That was awfully quick," Harper notes. "Doesn't it take a lot longer?"

"Yes, it does. Sometimes weeks. But they aren't analyzing the DNA at this point. There was a wallet in the pocket of the girl's jeans with Hailey Ann Santiago's driver's license. Also, her missing-persons file mentioned an appendectomy scar and a belly ring with a dolphin on it. Both were on the corpse. It's Hailey. I'm sure of it." Oliver hangs his head and wipes away what appears to be a tear.

I'd do the same, but I think I'm cried out. I do send prayers and sympathies out to Mr. and Mrs. Santiago, imagining what they must be going through, knowing their daughter will never come home again. Much like my Emily. How many years did my grandparents search for her? When did they give up? At least Hailey will have a proper burial and a final resting place that isn't a foot of dirt and leaves.

Mary approaches me. "I'm very proud of you, Kendall. I know you had some hesitation when you got here at the beginning of the week. Look how far you've come. You're not just ghost hunting or cleansing people's houses, you're giving families closure. You have to keep putting yourself out there. It's what God wants you to do."

I listen intently to the small woman who so believes in me. "I will, Mary. I promise."

I have to get my ghost-huntress team back together and we have to keep assisting those who reach out to us. Life itself is one big walking risk. Sure, there may be a Sherry Biddison around the corner here and there. I might be hit by a MARTA train one day too. You never know. I am sure of one thing— something Loreen told me not too long ago: if I give in, then the bad guy wins. The bad guy being the woman who tried to kill her own daughter-in-law (Sherry) or the mucked-up boyfriend who murdered Hailey.

I reach to hug Mary, but she pulls back. "No, no, dear, that's all right. That's what I'm here for."

Geesh . . . touchy much?

"I think you deserve some rest," Mary says with a sweet smile. She looks at everyone else. "You all do. Why don't we break for a while?"

"Good idea," Oliver says. "Let's go eat."

I weave my way up the stairs feeling like there's a ball and chain attached to me. I've never been so tired in my whole life, yet I'm also exhilarated that we found Hailey. The fact that there may be justice in all of this is an amazing high. No drug could ever feel like this.

In the kitchen, I fill my plate with lunchmeats, salad, and fruit, and then I go out into the sunshine of the front courtyard for a breather on my own while everyone else settles around the large table. Fifteen minutes later, I'm full as a tick, so I lean back into the chaise longue and luxuriate in the sunshine, feeling quite at peace. Soon, the air carries an unfamiliar song tiptoeing along with the breeze. Hmmm . . . Patrick is somewhere playing his guitar. I follow the melody through the front garden and down the long steps to the backyard. He's sitting on the edge of the hot tub, strumming away barehanded, his feet dangling in the water. Now, that's quite a change!

"Well . . . look at you," I say as I sneak up on him and then sit down on the rim of the Jacuzzi.

He doesn't jump or anything, though. I'm sure he sensed my arrival. Continuing to pluck at the strings, he says, "Yeah, well, I don't seem to be so skeeved out by water anymore. There was this cute chick trying to drink in the entire Pacific Ocean yesterday and I had to leap in and save her. Sort of . . . got over my phobia."

A skitter of excitement runs up and down the length of my back when I hear him refer to me as "this cute chick." I totally want to geek out at this moment, but instead I scrutinize the tattoo on his biceps that's peeking out from his T-shirt.

"What's the deal with the smirking ghost?" I ask.

Patrick lifts his sleeve. "I don't know. Seemed like a good idea. I see spirits and hear them, so I thought if I made light of it, they might go away. Now I know they're part of me and my future. You should get one too."

I toss my head back. "Me? A tattoo? Right. Like my mom wouldn't go totally postal over that!"

"We'll go to the airport together and we'll stop at a place. Wha'd'ya say?"

"I think you've definitely lost it!" I bend forward to get a good look at his face. "Seriously, though ... I'm proud of you, Patrick. You know, for accepting your abilities. No matter how you got them, they're part of you now."

"Thanks, Kendall. It's still a little discombobulating. I'll get used to it, though. Knowing there are others like me makes me feel less of a freak."

"Oh, come on," I say with a laugh. "We're all freaks."

His laughter bubbles up from his chest and breaks forth, and he gives me a huge smile that makes my knees weak. "I suppose we are."

My hands shake a bit and I grip them together as I speak. "The most interesting thing through all of this is that you and I have this sort of infused energy between us when we connect. I mean, I've seen a lot of stuff since my awakening. A lot.

Mostly things about other people. I've never been able to pick up anything about myself—other than in dreams. It just seemed that with this case, we saw more with each other than we did apart, and I can't explain that." God, I'm rambling like an idiot.

He twists his head and his delicious brown eyes move over my face. "We have something . . . special, Kendall."

My head drops and my hair covers my face, hopefully hiding a massive blush. Attraction and flirtation aside, I need to ask a very selfish question.

Patrick moves in close. "You want me to help you with something?"

I sit back slightly and rock on my hands. "Yeah. I do. I want to find out what we can see together about my birth mother, Emily, and any information on her parents, my grandparents. I mean, I've gotten snippets of names and license plates, but nothing definitive enough to say *that* is where they are and *this* is how I can find them."

He sets his guitar aside and adjusts to face me. He spreads his hands out on his lap, palms up. I place mine in his and our fingers entwine. Immediately, I feel like I'm flying through a wormhole in time as our minds join in search of Emily Jane Faulkner and my grandparents. Spiraling and twisting through multiple memories that belong to neither of us, we come to a halt at the edge of a tranquil lake. Little St. Germain Lake, in Wisconsin, just like Emily's license plate read. There, she sits on a pontoon boat fishing with an older man. She's about my age and she's laughing and cutting up. The man is her father, John

Thomas Faulkner, and he's found a lake turtle that he's hauling in with the net. A woman with short salt-and-pepper hair sits nearby sipping homemade lemonade, egging them both on. It's Emily's mother, my grandmother Anna Wynn Faulkner. I try not to allow my personal feelings to amp up at this moment as I focus on the visions before us.

Our hands tighten and the visualization adjusts in a whooshy kind of way, like fast-forwarding a movie as quickly as possible. We're no longer in Wisconsin, but we're still next to a lake. A gorgeous, breathtaking, amazing, crystal-clear calm lake surrounded by the most fantastic scenery I've ever seen. Villas line the coast, which is covered with lazy trees. There are my grandparents. Much older than in my previous images of them. They're holding hands and sitting in . . . a gondola?

Where are they? I ask Patrick in my mind.

Looks like Naboo.

There's no such place.

He snickers at me. *I'm telling you, it looks like Queen Padmé Amidala's home planet in the Star Wars movies. Naboo . . .*

OMG! I huff a surprised breath. God bless Celia Nichols and her penchant for useless trivia. One Saturday night when we had no ghost hunt planned, we hung out at her house watching torrents of the new Star Wars movies. She told me how they'd filmed the scenes for Naboo in Italy, in the lake country.

Lake Como? I ask Patrick. *Does that sound right?*

That's it! That's where these people are.

My grandparents are in Italy? Holy Roman Catholic Church! How in the world will I ever get to them?

We'll find a way, Kendall.

I like that "we" part.

My eyes open and I realize that my cheeks are wet from crying. Happy tears, though. Joy that I know where my grandparents live. That they live. Period. Bliss that Patrick was able to help me clarify this information. Hope that I might find them. Wishfulness that Patrick and I can make *this* work between us.

His hand lifts and brushes away my tears ever so gently. His dazzling eyes dance over me and we smile together.

"Thanks for that," I say. "And thanks again for saving my life."

He moves closer. He smells of Aquafresh and deodorant . . . and yumminess. "Thanks for saving mine, Kendall."

Our heads inch closer and closer together, like two magnets drawn toward each other. When his lips touch mine, I almost want to scream. It's the most magically soft, romantic, and sexy kiss I've ever had in my seventeen years. Patrick wraps his arms around me and pulls me to him, deepening the kiss. Mmm— this is a much better version than I experienced in my near-death experience. I never want this to stop.

I drape myself against Patrick and hold on for dear life, kissing him back with all my might.

And here I thought Jason Tillson could kiss.

Umm . . . Jason who?

Chapter Twenty-three

"Well, this is our last group session," Oliver says a few hours later. I've hot-tubbed, slept, and eaten the best turkey sandwich I've ever had in my life—and I'm in love again. Sad to think that this will all end tomorrow.

Don't think about it, Kendall . . .

Turning my attention to Oliver, I see him flash a real picture of Hailey Santiago from the overhead projector. "I wanted you to see the young woman you helped bring closure to. This is her senior picture, taken last fall. She would have been graduating this May and going off to Washington State University. 'So wise so young, they say do never live long.'"

Ahhh, another Shakespeare fan. I knew I liked Oliver.

"One of the officers shared with me that they found some DNA evidence under her fingernails that may lead to the killer. They also put out an all points bulletin for her ex-boyfriend Derrick Ingram, who fits the description in your visions and the pictures. They can't arrest him based solely on psychic information; however, they can bring him in for questioning,"

Oliver informs us. "In fact, they have a lead on his last known address and are making a visit to it as we speak." Oliver shakes his head as we all gasp, whoop, high-five, and mourn.

"At least Hailey's family can have a service for her now," Erin says quietly.

"That they can," Oliver says. "I think we've all learned some pretty amazing things this week. If you weren't enlightened before, you certainly are now."

"I don't wanna leave," Greg shouts out.

"Me either," says Carl and Ricky, followed by each of the Pucketts.

"That's an incredible compliment," Oliver says proudly. "I'll be sure to pass that along to the counselors."

Jessica raises her hand. "Speaking of that . . ."

"Yes, Jess?"

"I'm really curious about something. Except for Wisdom Walker at the sweat lodge, the counselors don't seem to leave this room or hang out around the inn. What's their deal? Are they just totally unsociable?"

Oliver tents his fingers in front of him. "Why don't you all meditate on that and see what you come up with?"

They don't come to meals. They don't sleep here. Come to think of it, their clothing never changes. Why didn't I notice that before? (Because I was preoccupied with Hailey, with Patrick . . . with myself.) They aren't touchy. They come and go like specters. *Whoa*. My eyes flutter closed, but it's not long before the clouds of understanding part in my mind and the answer to Jess's question is written in the blue sky.

"Oh my God!" I sputter. "They're ghosts?"

"That's impossible," Greg says. "I wouldn't be able to see them if they were."

Oliver smiles. "Think again, Greg."

Wisdom Walker, Peggy, Mary, and Heidi all file into the room. Spreading his hands wide, Oliver says, "I want you to meet my *own* spirit guides, who helped educate me through my own awakening. They have given of themselves to help me teach others to be aware of their talents and God-given abilities."

Jessica nudges me hard. "Holy shit, Kendall. I *can* see dead people!"

My eyebrows shoot up. "Who knew?"

It all makes sense now. I definitely think my parents got their money's worth sending me here to this retreat. It's the best spring break evah!

The next day, Jess crams the last of her shirts into her duffle bag and turns to me.

"I'm going to miss you, Kendall."

"Awww . . ." I rush to her side of the room and hug her tightly. "We'll totally keep in touch! And you'll have to come to Georgia and visit me."

"Can't we go somewhere cooler?" Jess teases.

I smack her and return to my own packing. "It's definitely been . . . an experience."

"You can say that again. And you and Patrick? Seems like that pink aura is just radiating off you."

My skin warms, giving me away. "You nailed that one too."

Jess claps her hands and jumps up and down. "I knew it!"

"Okay, already!"

She bounds for our cabin door. "I'm gonna go up to the kitchen and get a couple of sodas and Popsicles for us."

"That sounds awesome! Thanks!"

The door slams and I go back to folding my clothes. A moment later, I hear the door creak again. "Did you forget some—"

It's not Jessica.

"H-H-Hailey . . . it's you."

She walks toward me, no longer dirty and wearing torn clothes. Her hair is clean and brushed, and the bruises on her neck have disappeared.

"I wanted to thank you, Kendall. You and all of your friends. You found me."

"I did what I could, Hailey."

"You brought my family peace. Now I can finally rest."

"I'm so sorry for what happened to you." Gulping at the lump in my throat, I do my best not to cry again. "Hailey, do you see the light?"

"I do now. Since early this afternoon. I heard the police are looking for Derrick. Once he knows they've found my body and hears that his skin is under my nails, he'll confess. He has nothing else he can do but come clean."

"How can you be so blasé about him?" I ask, my anger rising at the killer.

Hailey smiles sweetly. "Because I'm of the light, Kendall. There's no judgment, hate, resentment, jealousy—these words are unknown to us in the light. Only when one can forgive can one truly advance as a being of the light. And I'm ready for that. I forgive him for what he did to me."

"Forgive him? Are you crazy? That asshole strangled you and left you in a national park!" I scream.

"Karma will come back on him, Kendall. I believe that."

"I don't buy it."

"It's difficult to explain this to the physical realm, but someday you'll understand, Kendall."

I hope that day is a long, long, long frickin' way away. A tear slips out of the corner of my eye, but I pay it no heed. "I'm sorry your life ended so early, Hailey. You will find peace in the light."

"I know," she says. "I'm so glad you came here. They said you were the one."

"Who is this *they*?" I ask in a shaky voice.

"Those on the other side who are still connected with you . . . with everyone. They knew your heart was pure and that you would do the right thing, which you did. I can join my grandparents and my aunt Morgan, who are waiting for me. I just had to thank you in person."

Hailey blows a kiss at me and then disappears.

I *did* do the right thing.

"I have never seen so much food in my entire life!" Maddie Puckett exclaims.

I have to agree. "Me either."

Before us, in the backyard of the inn, is a gigamonic smorgasbord. It's Saturday night, and this is our going-away party. Music is cranked and food is everywhere. A small bonfire roars, orange fingers dancing up to the sky. The smell of barbecued ribs, chicken, and brisket fill the air to go along with vats of coleslaw, potato salad, macaroni and cheese, and homemade baked beans. Chris and Glenn know how to put out a spread.

"Don't be shy, ladies," Glenn says from his position at the pit. "Plenty to eat."

"So much for dieting over spring break," Willow says.

"No way," I say. "I'm eating my weight in ribs tonight!"

We all mill around, laughing and swapping e-mail and Facebook addresses, promising to stay in touch. The digital world makes it easy for us to keep those promises.

"Don't you want my e-mail?" I hear from behind me.

I spin around and there stands Patrick, more handsome than I've ever seen him. He's wearing a black short-sleeved polo and tan cargo shorts, showing off muscular arms and legs. I can totally see that he was an outdoorsy guy before his near drowning. I hope he gets back to that—especially the diving that he loves so much.

"I most certainly want your e-mail. And your cell phone and your Facebook and Twitter—"

Patrick chuckles. "I've only got a cell and e-mail."

After we switch digits, he stashes his phone in his pocket and then takes my hand in his. There's no flash of shared information or a psychic connection this time. Just a boy holding the hand of a girl he likes. A girl who likes him back.

We pile our plates high with food and find a table away from the rest of the group. Patrick feeds me pineapple, and it's like I'm some Greek goddess being worshiped by her faithful manservant. Okay, not that I think Patrick's, like, my manservant ... it just feels so decadent. It's natural and oh, so right.

His eyes never leave my face and his smile never falters. We have changed each other. For the good. I'm no longer afraid of every psychic connection I have. And he's no longer scared of his own abilities. We were meant to be at this retreat together.

"I'm really going to miss you," I say, taking the first step.

He traces his forefinger over my hand. "I'm going to miss you too. I'm really stuck on you, Kendall Moorehead."

Siiiiiiiiiiiigh. "Too bad you live in Florida."

"Too bad you live in Georgia," he mocks.

I take a bite of the yummy rib and munch on it quickly. "It's not like we live a world apart. We've got the Internet, texting, the phone, and I'm sure we can visit each other. Summer will be here before we know it."

He hugs me to him and kisses me on the forehead. "You're beyond adorable, you know that? I've never met anyone like you."

"Is that a good thing?" I ask with my eyebrow raised.

"It's a *very* good thing." He tugs me so close that our hips and thighs touch on the bench. "I'm not letting you get away from me anytime soon."

Swoooooon.

Is this what it means to find your equal? Your soul mate? And can it possibly happen so young?

I don't need the answer right now. I only need to enjoy the time I have left with Patrick before we both wing back to the East Coast and our real worlds.

Ricky hops up and starts dancing, pulling Jess to her feet. They crunk out together in the funkiest way to the festive music. Chris, Glenn, and Oliver clap along and others get up and join in the party. Josiah and Willow move to the rhythm, and then I see everyone part to make way for Micah.

"What does he have?" I ask Patrick.

It's something on a string and it's on fire. WTF?

"Awesome!" Patrick exclaims. "It's poi dancing. I saw this when my dad and I were in the Philippines. Let's go watch."

"It's what?"

"Fire dancing," Patrick says. "It's a ball of fire suspended from a strip of rope or a chain. You spin it around in patterns and stuff. It's amazing."

Patrick grabs my hand and pulls me along. Loud disco music streams from the house speakers and everyone is moving to the beat. Micah is twirling the fire balls on strings around his feet in circular patterns. I keep thinking he's going to burn himself, but he knows exactly which direction to move in to keep the fire in check.

"Woooo!" I shout out, clapping along.

"Be right back."

Patrick hops into the middle with Micah and selects a couple of poi balls, lighting them from Micah's. Patrick twirls and rotates them in all sorts of cool patterns. He weaves and wraps and makes a butterfly formation and then ends with so many circles that it looks like the Olympic rings. At the end, he and Micah stamp out the poi fire and then high-five and fist bump each other. Absolutely breathtaking!

"You guys should take that on the road," Jess suggests.

Micah hugs her and says, "You should see me with glow sticks."

"That was incredible," I say to Patrick and reach up to kiss him. He lowers his head to mine and smacks me soundly on the mouth.

The disco hit "We Are Family" from the 1970s sounds out and we all—even the La'Costons and Oliver—take to the improvised dance floor, grooving and swinging with each other. I hold hands with the most unbelievable guy I've ever met and I'm surrounded by people who were complete strangers just a week ago. However, our shared talents and abilities brought us together for a reason. We formed an alliance to do good. Our own version of Super Friends . . . only Super Psychics.

I know my mission in life. No longer am I afraid, timorous, or frightened. God will watch out for me. Anona will watch out for me. All of my friends will watch out for me. The ones I have back home, the ones who've moved to Alaska, and the ones I've met here. I'll never give in to bad spirits and I'll never let them win.

Patrick swings me around and then cuddles me in his arms. "You are so amazing. The most beautiful girl I've ever met. I've never known anyone braver. You're my heroine."

My heart is totally going to melt into a pile of goo. Patrick's lips touch mine in a thrilling moment and I know I've found *my* hero.

Epilogue

Delta flight number 1812 is on final approach to Hartsfield-Jackson Atlanta International Airport, and I can't stop rubbing my left arm. The airport limo came to get Patrick and me this morning at the Rose Briar Inn—we shared a ride this time—he had them take a detour to Anonymous Tattooing Company so I could get a small ghost to match his. A dude named Zack was very careful in explaining the process and inking on the smirking specter.

Patrick and I call him Boo! Mom will freak, but she'll just have to get used to it.

When the wheels go down on the tarmac, I begin to sense a melancholy creep over me. I'm going to miss Patrick . . . and all of my new friends, although I know we'll keep in touch. But when the plane slides up to the gate, I'm actually a little relieved to be home. I missed Celia and Becca and even Kaitlin, the little brat, and I can't wait to get back into the routine of school, homework, and ghost hunting.

I scoot through Concourse B, resisting the urge for a Chick-fil-layover, and hop the tram. The escalator is slow, so I begin climbing it like a staircase. When I emerge at the top, there stand Mom, Dad, and Kaitlin with a WELCOME HOME, KENDALL sign in their hands. I'm swooped into their arms for a gigantic Moorehead group hug. While these aren't my "real" parents, they are the people who have loved and raised me and continue to take care of me. I am a part of them and they're a part of me.

The whole time we're at baggage claim, Kaitlin prattles on about her soccer camp and how her team took the cup. I try to act interested, but all I can think of is a promise I made nearly a week ago.

"Mom?" I ask sheepishly as I tug on her sleeve. "Do you mind if we make an out-of-the-way stop before we go home? It's something I *have* to do."

Her gentle face tenses momentarily, but she knows it must be something I have to do. "Of course we can, dear."

Forty-five minutes later, we stop at the quaint house of Lindsey Wright in Lawrenceville, Georgia. I have to deliver the message of love that Richie, her fiancé, gave me on the airplane. It's the right thing to do.

Ding-dong.

A pretty brunette answers the door. "Yes? May I help you?"

Deep breath for fortification. "You're Lindsey and I'm

Kendall." I extend my hand in a very grown-up way; Lindsey accepts it. "Please don't think I'm some kind of wackjob. I'm a psychic medium and I had a conversation with your Richie a week ago."

Lindsey's face pales and she steps aside to let me in.

"Please sit," she says. "I've had a couple of psychics contact me. Not one so young . . . or bold."

I sit on the brown suede sectional and cross my ankles. I explain my interaction with Richie on the airplane and how I helped him pass into the light. Lindsey breaks into tears and reaches for a Kleenex.

"I'm sorry to upset you, but he was insistent that I give you two very important messages."

Lindsey chortles through her tears. "That sounds like Richie."

I take out my notebook and read from it. "Lindsey, Richie wanted me to tell you that he loved you more than anything and that knowing you and being with you made his life complete."

I pause, feeling the poignancy of his words clog in my throat. Lindsey dabs her eyes and smiles through her tears. "Thank you for that, Kendall."

"There's one more thing," I explain. "He bought you a black pearl necklace from eBay, from the family of a World War Two veteran who got them in Japan. He hid it in the house and it was to be your wedding present."

Her hand covers mine. "This is a real test. Do you know where he said it was?"

I gulp hard. "In the attic, by the windowsill."

Lindsey leaves me and I stare at a picture on the mantel. It's of the man I encountered on the plane, the sweet young woman curled against his side. Richie and Lindsey.

Overhead, I hear a bit of tromping around, and then Lindsey comes barreling down the stairs. "Oh my God, Kendall! You're the genuine article! Look!"

She pulls open the velvet case and within the softness sits a necklace of perfectly matched black pearls. Lindsey clutches it to her heart. "I can't thank you enough for this . . . and most of all, for Richie's last words. I will treasure them always."

We hug and I say goodbye. No need for me to linger. My work here is done.

Celia's eyes grow round as marbles. "I can't believe you just walked up to her door, knocked, and said 'Hey, I had a convo with your dead fiancé.' Damn, K, you've got balls."

I smack at Celia across her bed, where we're both sitting. "I did what I had to do. It was the right thing."

She rams her hands into her black hair. "That's incredible!" Then the smile runs away from her face. "Why haven't you been answering my text messages?"

I shake my head. "So sorry—I've been consumed with this whole Hailey Santiago case. You know, the girl you sketched for Patrick and me."

Celia gets a knowing smile. "Oh, yeah, cutie pie. What's his deal?"

"No deal. We're . . . connected."

Celia snickers. "Is that what the kids are calling it these days? I suppose hooking up with some hottie like him was a lot more important than watching the old BlackBerry for crucial messages from your best friend."

"What*ever*," I say. "What was so urgent?"

"My cousin Paul says that John and Anna Faulkner are presently out of the country, according to his sources."

"Right," I say. "They're in Italy."

"How do you know that?" she asks, stunned.

"Ummm . . . I'm psychic?"

Celia shakes it off. "Okay, there's more. Paul found the Andy Caminiti from your vision, the one who was thought to be in the car with Emily when she died."

"Crappity-crap, Cel! That's huge! You should have called and told me."

She holds me off. "I'm telling you now, dude!"

"Right—so?"

"Turns out that an Andy Caminiti *was* Emily Jane Faulkner's boyfriend and may have been in the car with her the night of the accident. He went missing seventeen years ago—no body, nothing."

I drop my head. "But you just said your cousin found him."

"My cousin found a her," Celia says.

"I'm confused."

"You may have seen it incorrectly in your vision. It's not Andy, it's Andi, with an *i*. As in short for Andrea. Andrea Caminiti."

"A woman?"

Celia nods and adds a *duh* for good measure. "Andy and Andrea Caminiti were twins. So maybe she can tell you something about him."

Now I get it! "Where does she live?" I ask.

"St. Louis."

I sag into the down cushion of Celia's bed. "Damn . . . that's not close." But it is closer than Italy. First, I'll find my father, then I'll find my grandparents.

Celia smiles knowingly. "Well, St. Louis or not, she might know who your father is."

I think I'm going to pass out.

And on the way home from Celia's, as I'm shaking like a leaf, I get a text message that rocks my world even more. It's from Patrick and it reads:

>K - Dad getting transferred. Moving to Dobbins AFB, Marietta, GA. C u soon. <3 P

Now I'm *really* gonna pass out.

To be continued . . .

DISCLAIMER

The thoughts and feelings described by the character of Kendall and her friends are typical of those experienced by young people awakening to sensitive or psychic abilities.

Many of the events and situations encountered by Kendall and her team of paranormal investigators are based on events reported by real ghost hunters. Also, the equipment described in the book is standard in the field.

However, if you are a young person experiencing psychic phenomena, talk to an adult. And while real paranormal investigation is an exciting, interesting field, it is also a serious, sometimes even dangerous undertaking. I hope you are entertained by the Ghost Huntress, but please know that it's recommended that young people do not attempt the investigative techniques described here without proper adult supervision.

BIBLIOGRAPHY

Quote from Aldous Huxley from *The Little Giant Encyclopedia of Inspirational Quotes,* by Wendy Toliver, Sterling Publishing Company, Inc.

History of psychics, aura color definitions, and eagle totem information from *Picture Yourself Developing Your Psychic Abilities: Step-by-Step Instruction for Divination, Speaking to Spirit Guides, and Much More,* by Tiffany Johnson, Course Technology Books.

Legend of the Wampus Cat from *Spooky South,* retold by S. E. Schlosser, Globe Pequot Press.

Shakespeare quotes from www.enotes.com/shakespeare-quotes.

Information on cryptozoology from www.cryptozoology.com.

Information on traditional Native American sweat lodge ceremonies from en.wikipedia.org/wiki/Sweat_lodge and actual experiences from various Native American friends who have participated in sweats over the years.

Sioux prayer was printed in the *Los Angeles Times* to observe World Day of Prayer, in 1958. It comes from Cabot's Old

Indian Museum in Desert Hot Springs, California, and the author is unknown.

Animal totem information on dolphins from www.religions-and-spiritualities-guide.com.